St Elizabeth

Dealing with sic
funny, and up

This series takes a look at a hospital set up
especially to deal with such children,
peeping behind the scenes into almost all the
departments and clinics, exploring the
problems and solutions of various diseases,
while watching the staff fall helplessly
in love—with the kids and with each other.

Enjoy!

A New Zealand doctor with restless feet, **Helen Shelton** has lived and worked in Britain and travelled widely. Married to an Australian she met while on safari in Africa, she recently moved to Sydney where they plan to settle for a little while at least. She has always been an enthusiastic reader and writer and inspiration for the background for her medical romances comes directly from her own experiences working in hospitals in several countries around the world.

Recent titles by the same author:

Poppy's Passion
A Surgeon's Search
A Matter of Practice
Contract Dad
One Magical Kiss
An Unguarded Moment
A Surgeon for Susan
A Timely Affair
Idyllic Interlude
Courting Cathie*
Heart at Risk
The Best Man*

*Bachelor Doctors

KISSING
KATE

HELEN SHELTON

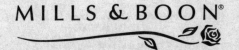

MILLS & BOON®

First published in Great Britain 2000
Harlequin Mills & Boon Limited,
Eton House, 18-24 Paradise Road, Richmond, Surrey TW9 1SR

© Poppytech Services Pty, Ltd 2000

ISBN 0 263 82433 0

Set in Times Roman 10½ on 11½ pt.
112-0010-51002

Printed and bound in Spain
by Litografia Rosés S.A., Barcelona

CHAPTER ONE

'Now, you haven't forgotten you've agreed to anaesthetise for my extra list tomorrow, have you, Kate?'

Kate, busy listening to the stethoscope she'd taped earlier to her baby patient's chest, barely caught the surgeon's words first time round. But when he repeated them, stressing her name this time in a gritty way, she looked up, struggled out from under the rail supporting the sterile guards covering her patient, tugged her ear pieces out of her ears and blinked vaguely at him. 'What?'

'My list. My extra theatre list?' The surgeon, looking up briefly from his field, exchanged a narrowed, meaningful look over Kate's head with the ODA—anaesthetic technician—who was helping Kate with the anaesthetic. 'Tomorrow? At two? I'm starting with that baby we were talking about yesterday with the pyloric stenosis.' He looked exasperated. 'Don't give me that innocent look, you wench. If you've forgotten, you're in trouble. Knowing what a flea brain you are, I even reminded you twice last week *and* I sent you a memo last Friday.'

Kate clicked her tongue, some vague recall of that filtering into her consciousness. Only remembering about the list didn't make it any easier for her to fit it in. 'Ah.'

He looked up to the ceiling as if begging for help. 'What does ''ah'' mean?'

5

'Ah means ah,' she said gingerly. 'I am a flea brain. Sorry, Giles. I forgot.'

'Why am I not surprised?' His shaggy eyebrows waggled at her above his blue surgical mask, then he looked up at the rest of the theatre. 'Is there anyone,' he said loudly, 'anyone at all, in this theatre, who does not remember me reminding Dr Lamb on at least two separate occasions about my special list this week?'

'Sorry, Kate.' Marie, the scrub nurse for the session, was laughing and she wasn't the only one.

'I can't believe you forgot!' Giles' registrar exclaimed.

'He must have told you ten times,' the circulating nurse added, with a giggle. 'I just about told him to shut up myself after the last time.'

'Mind like a lettuce,' Giles proclaimed. 'It is a source of constant amazement to me, Kate, that you manage to be so extraordinarily good at your job. You've booked yourself up to the hilt as usual with something else, I suppose?'

Friday was the one day of the week Kate didn't, generally, have herself fully scheduled in advance but unfortunately she'd already agreed to do other things the next day. 'I've got a full list in the morning plus I'm supervising one of the registrars' lists at the same time,' Kate confirmed weakly. They were lucky enough to have mainly very experienced registrars on the current anaesthetic rotation at St Elizabeth's, but the younger doctors, although all proficient, still required close monitoring by the consultants and she'd agreed to take on the job the next day. Not for her own registrar, because John was scheduled to be with one of her anaesthetic colleagues in a pain clinic at that time, but on behalf of another colleague who needed to take a few hours off in the morning to attend an event at her son's school.

'After that I'm going to have to run away straight away because I'm giving the lunch-time lecture at the medical school,' she added quickly. 'Then I've got a registrar teaching session which will go on till at least three. I've got an afternoon pain clinic back here for the rest of the afternoon and I know for sure that that's full, so I wouldn't be able to get away even for half an hour, then from six o'clock I'm on call for intensive care—'

But reading the surgeon's resigned expression above the mask, she broke off. Giles didn't want to know her problems, she knew. He couldn't be more uninterested. He didn't care that it hardly felt as if she'd spent more than a few hours other than sleeping time in her flat in months. It didn't make any difference to him how busy her commitments kept her or how panicky she felt at times about the way her research projects seemed to be growing out of control. It didn't affect his life if it felt, to her, that in the last year there hadn't been a single night when she'd left the hospital in daylight.

Not that she was complaining. Because she definitely wasn't. In all fairness—although she did, reluctantly, deep inside her somewhere acknowledge that she had, probably, taken on too much this year— she still loved her life. She loved her job and she thrived on the urgent, exhilarating rush of being so busy all the time. She'd worked hard for a long time to get where she was. And now she was, finally, here—senior lecturer and consultant anaesthetist at one of the finest children's hospitals in the world— she wasn't about to give up one second of it.

But there were drawbacks. She did seem to occasionally, like now, forget about the odd thing she'd agreed to do. And she no longer had much of a life outside the hospital. And she certainly looked a wreck. Her skin lately was turning dry and fragile— doubtless from chronic exposure to the hospital's air-conditioning and lack of daylight—and her hair, longer and stragglier than she'd ever had it before, desperately needed a decent cut. But her lifestyle, even if it felt a little, at times like this, as if it might just be a tiny bit out of control, wasn't one she'd trade for anything.

But Giles wouldn't be caring about anything like that either, she acknowledged. All Giles cared about was having an anaesthetist for his theatre list the next day.

'I can't believe I even agreed to do your list,' Kate added desperately. 'I mean, I definitely haven't written it into my notebook. And these days I hardly have five minutes free a week—even my Fridays seem to be booked way in advance. I do have a distant memory of you talking about your list, but are you sure I actually agreed to gas for you?'

'Utterly sure,' he said curtly.

'Completely sure,' echoed his registrar.

'You did say yes, Kate.' Marie, passing Giles another swab, was laughing again. 'I don't know where your mind is these days, girl. You're like a dizzy butterfly, rushing about here, there and everywhere. You'll forget your own name one of these days.'

'It's Kate,' Kate said lamely.

Giles sent her a dark glare above his mask. 'So, *Kate*, what are you going to do about it?'

'I'll get you someone,' she promised weakly. Giles was one of the most senior surgeons at Lizzie's but she felt guilty now for letting him down rather than intimidated. She'd been anaesthetising for his lists for three years—he insisted on having her and created havoc if she wasn't routinely allocated to him—and beneath the brisk exterior she'd discovered he was soft as a marshmallow. She was very fond of both him and his wife, and she counted them amongst her friends.

'I swear I'll find you someone,' she insisted again. 'One of the other anaesthetists will be free. I'll get the duty one to cover you if I can't find anyone else. I'm sorry, Giles—'

'Get me Mark,' the surgeon said strongly.

Kate pulled a face. The thought of trying to persuade Mark to fill in for her wasn't a pleasant one. Not considering her fellow anaesthetist had already made his disapproval of her current workload clear on far more than one occasion lately. Given that they were friends as well as colleagues, she accepted Mark's criticism was well intentioned in that he was worried for her, but he'd definitely been testy the week before when she'd had to ask him to cover one of her lists when she'd found herself unexpectedly double booked.

'Actually, Giles,' Kate said carefully, 'I've just remembered that Tony Reynolds is probably free tomorrow—'

'No good.' Busy closing their patient's tiny wound now, the surgeon merely spared her a meaningful glare. 'I want the best, Kate, my darling. If I can't have you, I want Mark. You or Mark. Mark or you. Either way, makes no difference. I just want one of you.'

'I'll ask him,' she agreed wanly, not looking forward to it. 'But what if—'

'I don't want to hear a "what if".' Giles looked

stern. 'You or Mark, wench. I'm not operating on that baby with anyone else.'

Mark was happy with the way his anaesthetic list had gone that afternoon. They'd been busy—seven cases were a lot when every one of them involved a toddler needing coaxing and play for reassurance before he put him or her to sleep—but it was only just after five now and they were finished.

He did his usual routine post-list check of recovery, pleased to see all but his last child fully awake and apparently cheerful and ready to be transferred back to their wards.

'Any problems with this last one, I'll be in the staff room,' he told Siobhan, the recovery nurse looking after his final patient. He preferred not to leave the theatre area until all his patients were transferred to the ward. With adults it was possible to be more relaxed—if something went wrong there was more time—but with children, and as Lizzie's was a specialist children's hospital here he only had child patients, he never allowed room for risk.

A two-year-old who'd just had an inguinal hernia operation, the toddler seemed content enough, if too drowsy to make much of a fuss when Mark squeezed his legs gently. The monitor clipped to one of his toes showed his blood oxygen saturation level was entirely normal and Mark was happy with him. 'I think he's just lazy.'

'God give me more lazy children,' Siobhan joked, adjusting the child's oxygen mask slightly on his little face. 'I love them. Usually the normal ones are out of their cots and halfway down the hall by now.'

Mark smiled. He knew exactly what she meant. The noise level from his earlier cases was already growing more raucous. 'If he isn't a bit more lively in ten minutes give me a shout,' he instructed. It was probably the pain relief he'd given the child that was causing the drowsiness but he still wanted to look at him again if he didn't become more lively soon.

But he only got as far as the door out of Recovery before Lucy, one of the other recovery nurses, called him back. 'Don't you dare leave here without buying some of my chocolates, Mark Summers.' She dashed to the main nursing desk. 'You promised.'

Mark rolled his eyes. The nursing staff were selling boxes of chocolates to raise money for the hospital's planned new bone-marrow transplant unit. He didn't object to making the donation, but it was getting to the stage when he now owned enough of the chocolate to start his own shop. 'I'm ninety-nine per cent sure you're lying when you say I promised to buy these,' he objected mildly when Lucy came hurrying back to him bearing two more boxes. 'I've already dozens and I don't like chocolate.'

'Everyone likes chocolate,' Lucy countered briskly. 'And you haven't bought any from me before. You can't play favourites, Mark. Not you. You buy from one of us, you have to buy from all of us. You know that. This place will turn into a war zone if you start playing favourites with the nurses.'

'How about I just make a donation?' he ventured, signing the card she gave him to formalise his pledge since he was still wearing theatre blues and so didn't have his wallet on him.

'You have to take the chocolates,' she insisted, forcing them into his hands. 'That's the deal. We get the money and you get the chocolates. Besides, there're hundreds of boxes out there in the office. They're stacked floor to ceiling. We've got to get rid

of them so we can use the room again. You'll have
to give them to your current sweetheart if you can't
eat them yourself.'

'I don't have,' he pointed out, taking the chocolates
just to keep her happy, 'a current sweetheart. Lucky
these have got long expiry dates because you'll all be
getting these back come Christmas.'

Lucy looked surprised. 'We thought you were still
seeing that new ENT registrar. What's her name
again? The pretty one with the blonde hair. Is it
Janet—?'

'You thought wrong.' Mark tapped her nose,
lightly but pointedly. 'Not that it's any of your business.'

'Of course it's our business.' The nurse laughed.
'Any gorgeous, eligible man around this place is our
business. Hey, Siobhan!' She grinned at the other
nurse. 'Did you know Mark and that ENT registrar
have split up—?'

'We didn't *split up*,' Mark interjected. 'We weren't
going out.' The registrar had only recently begun at
Lizzie's and he'd felt sorry for her after a theatre session a few weeks before when her boss had spent the
entire three hours barking at her for an error that
hadn't been her fault. He'd taken her out for a drink
in an attempt to point that out and cheer her up.
Obviously they'd been seen. His mistake, clearly, had
been choosing a pub too close to the hospital. 'One
night, weeks ago, we had a couple of drinks—'

'She's not your type,' Siobhan declared sagely,
looking up from her little patient to shake her head
at him. 'I could have told you that the first day she
arrived if you'd bothered to ask me.'

Mark opened his mouth to ask why, on earth, he

would ever bother to do that, but Lucy got in before him.

'I think she's nice,' she protested. 'She seems very sweet.'

'*Too* sweet.' Siobhan seemed very sure. 'Too sweet and too young. Mark likes his women to have a bit more spark, don't you, Mark? You prefer a bit of a challenge.'

'It's your story, Siobhan,' Mark countered easily, retreating for the door. 'You tell me.'

There was coffee made in the percolator in the staff room and he checked to see that it was warm, then poured himself a mug and took it over to one of the chairs and sat himself down. Someone had left the current *British Journal of Anaesthesia* discarded on the table and he retrieved it, ran his eye down its list of contents, then opened it to an article that he saw had been co-written by one of his colleagues.

The sound of the door opening again a few minutes later brought his head up and he grinned. 'Hi!' He held up the journal. 'Look what I've found.'

'Is that the latest *BJA*?' Kate wrinkled her nose at him as she tilted her head to see the magazine's cover. 'I haven't had time to look at it myself yet. At least, I've proofed the article but I haven't seen the issue itself. What do you think? Too dry?'

'It's interesting,' he argued. Her study, one he'd already known about, detailed possible new applications for an established drug in paediatric anaesthesia. 'You know you write well.'

'I wasn't sure with that one.' She clicked her tongue. 'It was a rushed job. The Prof was supposed to help but went away without telling me and I had to write up the lot myself in one weekend. He didn't even look at it until after it was accepted.' She poured herself the last of the coffee. 'Actually, I'm glad I caught you. I had my fingers crossed you'd be here.'

'Why?' He sent her a suspicious look. Fond as he was of Kate, he knew her well enough to be wary. They'd trained as registrars together, although he'd always been a couple of years ahead of her, firstly at London's Guy's Hospital and later at Great Ormond Street and had been friends for years. She was radiant, funny and incredibly intelligent—even if there were times when the latter seemed hard to believe—and despite being young she was certainly one of the best anaesthetists on staff at St Elizabeth's.

But that didn't mean he was blind to her faults. And Kate had many. And when she looked at him like that, in that sweet little butter-wouldn't-melt-in-her-mouth way of hers, he'd come to understand that it was time to beware. 'What do you want?'

She looked offended. 'Why do you always assume that every time I come near you it's because I want something?'

He laughed. 'Come on, Kate. Be reasonable. You always do want something.'

'You obviously don't know me as well as you think you do,' she countered lightly. She came and sat opposite him, leaned back, crossed her lovely legs and regarded him solemnly. 'So…how are you?'

He put down the journal and folded his arms, electing to humour her. 'Fine.'

'How's work?'

She was tired, he realised. Really, deeply tired. It wasn't always easy to tell with Kate because both her striking fairness and her beauty—and she was beautiful—tended to distract the eye. But her skin, although still flawless, looked drawn and pale and the shadows under her eyes were deeper than usual. He worried for her as he always worried for her. She took on too much. She had always taken on too much—refusing to acknowledge her limitations was primary among her faults—but of course pointing that out to her again would be as utterly futile as it had ever been and for once he restrained himself from saying anything. 'Work's fine,' he answered carefully.

'Home?'

'Fine as well.'

'Janet?'

He frowned. 'What?'

'Janet Holmes,' she said delicately. 'The new ENT registrar. I heard you two were seeing a lot—'

'We're not,' he interrupted.

'Ah. I'm sorry.' She looked sympathetic. 'She seems very sweet. Are you all right—?'

'Fine.' He sighed. There wasn't any point in explaining. Kate wouldn't listen. She'd seem to listen but in reality her mind would be elsewhere, deliberating over some obscure point of physiology or contemplating what task she'd be dashing off to accomplish next, no doubt. 'Kate, is there a point to this?' he asked wearily. 'I mean, an actual point?'

'Oh, I just wanted to reassure myself that you were OK and everything,' she said airily, her gloriously green eyes so innocent that if he hadn't known her better he might even have believed her.

He leaned back in his chair and crossed his feet. 'I'm fine.'

'What are you up to this weekend?' Distracting him briefly again, she recrossed her legs the opposite way. 'Going down to the house?'

'After lunch tomorrow,' he confirmed. He'd been slowly, very slowly, restoring a cottage he'd bought several years before in Wiltshire. For him, it was the ideal retreat. Close enough to London to mean he could get there fairly effortlessly most weekends when he wasn't on call or wanting to stay in town, it was at the same time so utterly tranquil and isolated he invariably felt as if he'd been on a long holiday when he returned.

'After *lunch* tomorrow.' Kate looked interested. 'So you're taking tomorrow afternoon off, then?'

'Finishing at twelve,' he confirmed. Every second Friday afternoon he covered a cardiac surgery list but this week it had been cancelled because the surgeon he worked with and his registrar were attending a conference in Edinburgh. 'Why?'

'Oh, nothing much.' She inspected her nails. 'How would you feel about doing a list for Giles?'

He felt his eyes narrow. 'And you just happened to offer this because…? Hmm, Kate?'

'Know-it-all.' She poked her little tongue out at him. 'All right. All right,' she said cheerfully. 'You win. Yes, I do want something. I came looking for you because I'm desperate. I've mucked everything up. I'm really, really sorry, but Giles just demanded I ask you. I promise it'll only hold you up a couple of hours but I'm begging you, on my knees, Mark, please could you just do it for me?'

'You've double booked,' he said tiredly.

'Triple, really,' she admitted. 'Plus I agreed to be on call instead of Tim in ICU tomorrow night. I really don't understand how it happened—'

'It happened,' he said grimly, 'because you're stupid. Kate, for an intelligent woman you are the most stupid, pigheaded, stubborn—' He broke off on a curse. 'You can't keep going on like this.'

'I'm fine,' she insisted, looking startled by his outburst. 'I'm managing. Really. Stop worrying, Mark.

Everything will be fine if you could just do this one thing for me.'

'Only it's not one thing, Kate. Is it?' Angry now, not about her asking for help because he would always help, but with her for having taken on so much in the first place, he pushed his chair back and strode away from the table. 'It's never one thing. And it keeps going on and on.' He paused at the window, looking briefly out over the tranquil peace of Regent's Park, before spinning around again to glare at her. 'You're doing too much. You're hugely over-committed. I couldn't believe it when I saw the new roster for this quarter. You're doing too many lists, too much teaching and you've agreed to take on too much on-call work. I know you love your work,' he said swiftly when she opened her mouth, reading her, after all these years, effortlessly, 'but this insane. At this rate you'll be burnt out within another year. You're not looking after yourself.'

'I'm not that badly over-committed,' she argued. 'The main problem is my own disorganisation. If I had a bit more time I could make it work.'

'You don't have enough time.' He scanned her face irritably. 'There are only twenty-four hours in a day and only seven days in a week. That's not going to change, Kate. And look at you. Have you even looked in a mirror lately? You look like hell.' It was a lie. She looked exquisite, as she always did—tired, but exquisite—but he had to find something to break through her defensiveness. 'You're exhausted. When was the last time you took any time off?'

'I'm going to France in November.'

'That's more than six months from now,' he said grimly. 'And you're not going for a holiday, you're presenting at a conference.'

'I thought I'd take a couple of days—'

'Not long enough,' he declared. 'And not soon enough. You need a break, Kate. Be reasonable. Take a few weeks. A week even. Go somewhere hot, rest on a beach and unwind. You can't give the kids here your best when you're exhausted.'

'I will,' she promised, nodding firmly although that didn't make him any more inclined to believe her. 'As soon as I get some time. I promise. What about tomorrow?'

He shook his head, still not believing her but resigned to not being able to do anything about it. 'What time and where?' he asked wearily.

'Two, Theatre Four. There're four children on the list, two of them babies.' She retrieved a sheet of paper from the files she'd been carrying when she'd come into the room and came over to him with it. 'I've already been to the wards and seen them all. This first baby with pyloric stenosis is in the unit. She's a darling, you'll love her. Big blue eyes you would not believe.'

He went back to his chair and she sat on the arm of it leaning unselfconsciously against him while she ran through the details of the case. The pyloric stenosis—a thickening of the muscle surrounding the bottom of the stomach meaning food had trouble getting through—had gone unnoticed for several weeks after delivery. Since the baby hadn't developed the characteristic projectile vomiting immediately, the reason for her feeding difficulties had been delayed, the family GP having initially put the problems down to parental anxiety. By the time the baby had arrived at Lizzie's she'd been shocked and severely dehydrated, hence the reason she'd needed intensive care. The surgery itself for pyloric stenosis was relatively simple, basically just cutting through the extra muscle. What took time, invariably, was making the right diagnosis.

'Her blood tests aren't looking too bad today,' Kate finished. 'So she'll be fine tomorrow. Everything should be quite straightforward.' She ran her finger down the list. 'No other problems there. I'm sure you'll be out of there by five. Six at the latest. You know Giles. He's nice and fast.'

Mark nodded, endeavouring to concentrate on the sheet of names and procedures rather than on Kate's proximity. The other anaesthetist, he knew, both in theory and practice, didn't think of herself as a particularly sexual person. Probably as a consequence of that, it had always been very clear to him that she saw him solely as a friend rather than as a man. When they'd been junior doctors on the same ward together near the beginnings of their careers, that indifference had bothered him. But he was used to it now—in fact, rather than simply being used to it, he was happy with it.

Even contemplating any...deepening in their relationship was the height of folly as far as he was concerned. Kate drove him mad enough as it was.

Unfortunately, however, his senses were a little less co-operative since invariably there were times when he reacted to her as a lovely, physically desirable woman despite his brain's understanding that their relationship would always be strictly platonic. Now was one of those times, since the relaxed movement of her arm against his stirred impulses he'd rather have left unstirred.

'You're wearing scent,' he observed, irritated with the husky timbre of his voice.

'It's called "Kissing".' She looked pleased that

he'd noticed. 'It's a natural, herbal fragrance. The mother of one of my babies today sells perfumes door to door and I liked this one best. It was quite cheap actually so it wasn't such an extravagance.' She held her fine-boned wrist extended up to his nose. 'Do you like it?'

'It's OK,' he said neutrally, keeping his tone non-committal although he inhaled the warm, enticing fragrance appreciatively. The overt sensuality of her choice of scent surprised him. 'I thought you didn't like perfume.'

'She put it into a body lotion for me,' she revealed. 'My skin's been like sandpaper lately so I thought I'd better try something before it starts shredding off. You just smear this stuff on after a shower and it works like a moisturiser. It's nice stuff, quite soft and smooth.'

'Tell Giles I'll be there.' Mark rose to his feet, deliberately not allowing himself to contemplate the image of Kate smearing anything anywhere. 'Tomorrow.' He moved towards the door. 'I'm going to check on Recovery, then I'm off home.' He saw from the clock on the wall above the door that it was almost seven. 'Want a lift?'

Her flat was a hospital-owned one, close enough to Lizzie's for her to be able to walk to and fro in only a few minutes, but it was on his way home and he was happy to drop her off. But she shook her head. 'I won't be able to get away for a few hours,' she explained. 'I've got to prepare for a lecture I'm giving tomorrow and then there's some work I want to do in the lab so—'

'Kate,' he growled, his anger at her workload rekindling at her recitation.

She rolled her eyes. 'I'll leave early,' she promised.

'I'll get an early night. Just as soon as I finish here I'll go straight home.'

'Promise me you'll take the weekend off.'

'I'm on call.'

'Next weekend, then,' he compromised.

'I need to anyway.' Some of her hair had come loose from the fabric band in which it had been held and she gathered up the golden strands and tied it all back up again. 'I'm planning to take the Saturday and Sunday off at least so I can start collating my research stuff ready to write up my new paper.'

'Come down to the cottage. Come down and help me with the garden.' The following weekend included the first of May's bank holiday Mondays. He wasn't on call at all over the weekend and he knew from the roster that Kate was free too.

He couldn't remember the last time she'd been with him to Wiltshire. Not that year, certainly, and probably not for at least twelve months. 'Three days away will do you the world of good.' And he'd be there to make sure she didn't bring work with her. 'If you refuse,' he warned, knowing from her doubtful expression that she was about to try, 'then tomorrow's off.' It was a bargaining point and he was going to use it for her own good. 'If you say no, then Giles will have to find another anaesthetist for the list.'

'That's not fair,' she wailed, but he just waited, and eventually she pulled one of her faces at him. 'Next weekend,' she agreed finally. 'Slave-driver. Last time I came down with you, you had me up on ladders painting the ceilings. You'll have me more exhausted from digging your blasted garden than I would be in a month on call.'

Mark grinned. 'It'll be good for you,' he countered evenly. 'I promise.'

CHAPTER TWO

'AND this,' Kate said, crouching over one of her little charges on one of the surgical wards in the middle of the following week, 'is my special magical cream.'

'Magical?' The child's big brown eyes widened. 'Is it really magical?' she whispered.

'Mmm.' Kate, her examination finished now, applied a second smear of EMLA cream to her patient's little arm and covered it carefully with a transparent dressing. The cream contained a local anaesthetic which would penetrate the skin and anaesthetise it so that when she came down to theatre Kate would be able to insert a cannular painlessly in preparation for giving her anaesthetic. 'When you wake up, there'll be a bandage here like little Teddy's got,' she held up the bandaged bear she'd be bringing with her to Theatres, 'but you'll have a golden star on your other arm.'

'I can't wait,' the little girl asserted. 'I'm going to have an operation. A clown is coming to see me and a nice man is going to fix my leg. And I'm going to be six next year.'

'Yes, you are,' Kate agreed, exchanging smiles with the child's tense-looking mother.

'I'm going to be sleeping for the operation.'

'A lovely sleep,' Kate confirmed.

'It won't hurt me.'

'No.' Kate stroked the little girl's hair back from her face. The procedure she was having to realign a badly healed fracture was not a minor one, but as with all their children they took great care to keep them comfortable. As soon as the child was asleep, Kate was going to put in a caudal block—anaesthetic administered directly into the lower part of her back—to provide pain relief throughout the time of her operation and immediately afterwards for at least twenty-four hours. 'No of course it won't.'

'And Teddy's going to be with me all the time.'

'Yes.' Teddy would be taken away only after she was asleep and he would be waiting for her again in Recovery after her operation. Allowing toys, along with parents, into the theatre area, and porters dressing as clowns and television characters to take the children to Theatres were some of the ways they tried to entertain their little patients and make them feel less anxious. Kate coming to the ward in full theatre gear including a blue paper hat covering her hair, rather than her normal clothes, was designed to help that too, since it meant she'd still look familiar when the child arrived in the anaesthetic room.

'And Mummy will be with you after you wake up,' the child's mother said quickly, coming to take her hand. 'Will the surgery take very long, Dr Lamb? The young doctors this morning said an hour or so but one of the nurses seemed to think it might be much longer.'

'Around an hour, or perhaps a little under that, is right for the actual operation,' Kate explained. 'But Sally will be down in Theatres longer than that of course because we won't be bringing her back to the ward before she's properly awake.'

'I can't have anything to drink,' Sally told her.

Kate smiled. Keeping their pre-op children from eating or drinking was a significant problem even though at Lizzie's they were more relaxed about fast-ing time than hospitals which dealt with adults. Generally, rather than the six to eight hours of strict fast required for adults, here she and her colleagues allowed water or clear fluids for children up until four hours pre-op, and for infants three hours. But even that was sometimes hard to control since those children who were well enough to be mobile generally ate communally at the tables in the play room. Pre-op children were given a 'nil-by-mouth' bib to wear so no one would feed them accidentally and either a nurse or a parent was asked to be with them at all times until they were transferred to theatre. The system worked relatively well but they still had to delay or rearrange a list, perhaps once or twice a month, because a child managed to eat or drink something milky.

'Nothing more to drink until after the operation,' she agreed, smiling when Sally opened her mouth obediently so she could examine her teeth. In children especially it was vitally important to document missing or chipped teeth since that avoided unnecessary X-rays and explorations of chests and tummies if they were only noticed missing after the anaesthetic.

'I'll see you in a little while,' she promised when she'd finished her examination. The porters would be coming to fetch Sally for the afternoon list in about an hour. 'How's the magic cream going?'

Sally wrinkled her little brow. 'I think it's working,' she told her assessingly.

'Claire, I've charted EMLA cream for every case,' Kate told the nurse who was in temporary charge of the ward as she returned the children's drug charts to her. 'I've applied little Sally Robson's already so she's all set to go. I want the rest to have premeds. Just nasal midazolam, thanks.' The drug, similar to a sort of very-short-acting Valium, relaxed the children prior to coming down to Theatres and the pharmacy at Lizzie's delivered it to them in an easily administered nasal spray. 'Timmy needs to have some Ventolin an hour pre-op since he's had a couple of admissions for asthma. The others all seem fine.'

'Thanks, Kate.' Claire flicked through the charts, clearly familiarising herself with Kate's orders. 'They're a cheerful bunch this afternoon. Unlike the ones for tomorrow. A couple of them don't look very well at all and the rest are all miserable. The SHO's just having a look at one of them now. I heard Mr Hamilton's usual anaesthetist is away in the morning. Will you be covering for his list then tomorrow morning?'

'Mark Summers is, I think,' Kate told her. She was on call for anaesthetics the following day and she'd offered to cover the list for her colleague who was away attending a seminar at another hospital but Mark had apparently already agreed.

'Mark?' The nurse's brows rose. 'Oh, great. It's ages since we've seen him down here. We've all missed him. He's doing mainly cardiac now, isn't he?'

'Cardiac and some neurosurgery,' Kate confirmed, quickly writing up her history and examination findings including the status of Sally's teeth on the anaesthetic case sheet attached to her notes. Six months earlier the retirement of one of the other anaesthetists had meant they'd all shuffled around their lists and Mark had given up his orthopaedic lists to take on extra cardiac and one neurosurgery session. Cardiac surgery anaesthetics was his special interest although he had had several years' experience in neuro as well.

'How's he been? Last we heard, he was going out

that with that new ENT registrar. Janet something, isn't it?'

'Janet Holmes.' Kate flicked back through one set of notes to check a set of blood test results. 'She seems nice but he told me it didn't work out,' she said absently.

'Oh, good.' Claire grinned, apparently unrepentant, when Kate sent her a startled look in response. 'Well,' she said defensively, 'gives us all another chance, doesn't it?'

'Does it?' Kate blinked at her. 'You fancy Mark, then, Claire?'

'Do I *fancy* him?' Claire was bemused by the question. 'Kate, wake up. Open your eyes, you mad woman. You're in another world, you are. We don't just fancy Mark, we *love* him. We adore him. He's wonderful. We all dream about going out with Mark.'

Kate smiled, picturing Mark's reaction to hearing that. Disbelief, probably. Panic, possibly, if he did believe it. 'He is very good-looking,' she conceded. Normally fairly oblivious to such things, even she had noticed that. Mark's features were even and attractive and he was tall and dark and strong. His dark blue eyes could seem uncomfortably penetrating at times but she suspected most other woman probably found that sort of regard more intriguing than unsettling. 'And I know he's popular. But I didn't quite realise *that* popular.'

'Believe it,' Claire said fervently. 'I just can't believe he's not married yet. I mean, he must have women throwing themselves at him all the time.'

'Perhaps that's the problem?' Kate speculated idly. 'Too much variety.' She and Mark had been good friends for years, but they weren't close enough for her to be a confidante regarding his love life. She usually knew when he was dating someone, and that seemed to be fairly frequently, but only because she tended to hear about it at work. He rarely mentioned his girlfriends to her directly and unless they were on staff at Lizzie's she rarely met them.

She finished looking through the last of the files she held, then returned them to the pile on the shelf near the drug cabinet where Claire was sorting through the cupboards.

'You know, I'm surprised he's not married too,' she said slowly, now she'd had time to think about it. Mark was the sort of man whom women, in her experience, generally regarded as ideal husband material. He had a tendency to boss her about a little, of course, which grated on her at times, but he was also warm, kind, loving and generous. He loved kids, and her comment about him enjoying variety was unfair because it wasn't as if he took heavy advantage of his looks and played the field as widely as some men would have. And from the conversations they'd had over the years she knew that, unlike her, he hoped one day to marry and have children of his own. 'You're right,' she told Claire. 'It can't be because of lack of offers. I might ask him about it.'

'When you find out, tell me,' Claire said with a laugh. 'And if it's just because he's still looking for the perfect woman, then find out what she's supposed to be like. I don't mind working a little transformation with myself.'

'I'll let you know,' Kate said easily. Claire was an attractive, lively woman and a wonderful nurse. She was very popular with her patients and colleagues. Perhaps Mark had no idea she was even interested in him? A subtle word in his ear about the nurse might even be the beginning of something wonderful.

'I'll talk to him,' she promised. Her gaze swinging away, she caught sight of the mouse clock on the wall above the main ward station and grimaced. It was almost one and she still had to get to Intensive Care to review one of her patients from the day before and grab lunch before she needed to be in Theatres by quarter past. 'Too much chatter, not enough work,' she told the nurse quickly, breaking into a skip towards the door. 'I've got to dash. Bye, Claire. Thanks.'

Her surgical ICU case, Michael Billings, a little eight-year-old she'd anaesthetised for his abdominal surgery the day before, was doing well. He'd been taken off the ventilator and was conscious, although asleep now, and apparently comfortable. 'We'll keep him in the unit overnight and bring him back here after his next lot of surgery tomorrow morning,' the anaesthetic registrar covering ICU told her.

Kate nodded. Michael had been admitted as an emergency the week before, very unwell, shocked, with a tender abdomen and blood tests suggesting an inflamed pancreas. The organ's normal role included producing the insulin needed to metabolise carbohydrates like sugar and the enzymes needed for digestion, but in Michael's case the enzymes had broken loose and started digesting the pancreas itself.

Pancreatitis in children was rare and it was very rare for them to need open surgery for it, but in Michael's case he'd been so dangerously ill that the surgeons had felt they had to make certain of the diagnosis by opening his tummy and taking a direct look. In the event that was fortunate because some of the pancreas had proven to be irreversibly damaged and that, along with some adjacent bowel, had had to be removed. Since the inflammation and healing was still ongoing, every second or third day from now on until he was better he was going to have to come back to theatre so his surgeon could wash out his abdomen again to prevent further damage and infection.

They still didn't know the initial cause of Michael's illness. Sometimes pancreatitis was associated with mumps or with trauma—most commonly bicycle accidents where the bike handle went into the abdomen—but with Michael they had no answers yet. At Lizzie's they only saw a handful of cases a year and Michael's was the severest Kate had ever seen.

She charted the pre-medication, midazolam again, which she wanted him to have before coming to theatre the next morning. 'Is Mum or Dad here?' She would have liked the chance to talk about the anaesthetic with them.

'They've just popped out for lunch,' the younger doctor revealed.

'I'll call back after my list tonight,' Kate told her.

She'd noticed Mark at the main desk talking intently with the consultant in charge of the unit when she'd arrived, and now, on her way out, she merely nodded hurriedly to him, knowing she didn't have enough time to chat, but he caught up with her in the changing area outside.

'Going to Theatres?'

'Hi!' She smiled a quick greeting as she shrugged out of the gown she'd worn to cover her theatre clothes while visiting ICU. 'I am but via the shop.' Kate quickly soaped and rinsed her hands, then stood back to let him use the basin while she dried and collected her things from the small locker bay. 'I need to grab a sandwich.' There were several little shops in the ground floor foyer at Lizzie's and Mrs Lewis, who ran the flower and fruit shop, sold lovely cheese and pickle sandwiches. 'I'm finding lately I get a bit dizzy if I skip lunch before a long list. Thanks again for doing Giles' list last Friday, Mark. And thanks for offering to do that orthopaedic list tomorrow. I thought I'd be doing that one.'

'No problem.' He put an arm out as she was about to leave and held the door open for her. 'Looking forward to coming away this weekend?'

'I need to talk to you about that,' she called, hurrying off. She didn't have time now to say anything on behalf of Claire but she'd try and grab a chance later. 'I don't think this weekend's going to work after all.' She dared a quick look back, then rolled her eyes at the dark disapproval with which he'd greeted her revelation. 'I'm running late. Sorry, Mark. I'll give you a call later.'

Only she didn't need to call him because he was anaesthetising that afternoon in the theatre next to hers and so she met up with him in the staff room when her own team took their usual fifteen-minute break at three-thirty.

Kate only popped in, intending to grab a drink and take it to the anaesthetic office because she needed to discuss some roster changes with the manager there, but Mark came after her, cornering her in the corridor before she made it as far as the office.

'Kate, that was a big favour I did for you last Friday.'

'I know. I know.' Mark had his mask down around his chin, and she pulled hers down too. 'I'm really sorry. I know we had a deal but, Mark, this weekend's just going to be impossible for me. How about five weeks from now? I've looked it up in my diary and I can definitely take a break then. The garden will wait a few weeks, won't it? In the meantime I've just got so much—'

But his expression had turned impatient. 'No way, sweet pea. I'm not letting you get away with that. You're absolutely right that we had a deal. And I'm going to make sure you stick to it.'

'Mark, I wish I could. But—'

'Giles' list?' He lifted his brows. 'Didn't finish till seven. The little baby with the pyloric stenosis was complicated. She took much longer than Giles was expecting. By the time everyone was out of Recovery it was after eight and I didn't get home till nine. I missed a whole afternoon and night of my weekend for you.'

'OK, OK, I feel guilty,' she protested. 'Really, really guilty.' It was true. She did. 'But I'll make it up to you, I promise. I'll cover any list you want or I'll even dig and cart dirt for you an entire weekend if that's what it's going to take. Just…not this weekend.'

But he shook his head. 'We're leaving at six,' he said quietly. 'Tomorrow night. I'll pick you up at the flat. Bring some old clothes.'

'I only have *old* clothes,' she said raggedly. The last time she'd had time to shop for clothes had been…at least a year ago. 'Mark, I really can't afford to take the full weekend off. Saturday, perhaps, one day OK, but—'

'Kate, you are taking it.' His determined expression allowed no argument. 'You are having a full three-day weekend away from Lizzie's and there aren't going to be any more complaints.'

'I'll try and move things around,' she murmured reluctantly, compromising. 'But if I can't—'

'I will find you,' he said softly, 'wherever you are,

and I will put you in my car and kidnap you. Am I making myself clear, Kate, my darling?'

'Crystal,' Kate said delicately, staring up at him, blinking her bemusement at his very stern, blue regard. 'I've always thought you bossy but you never used to be overbearing.'

'It's my new image.' He grinned. 'This is going to be good for you. Think of your mental health.'

'That's why I'm worried,' she grumbled. 'I haven't had three days away from Lizzie's in two years. What if my brain conks out?'

'What brain?' He dropped his arm meaning she could duck free of him. 'You're already a walking zombie.'

Agnes Coffee, the manager in the anaesthetic department office, looked pleased, at least, to see her. 'Oh, Dr Lamb,' she said, greeting Kate with a big smile, 'I was hoping you'd stop by. The Professor's had to leave early today but he did want me to ask you if you could look after his students tomorrow. He's taking tomorrow off, you see, before the long weekend. He's driving down to Southampton this afternoon. He did,' she slowed now, as if seeing Kate's hesitation, 'well, he certainly did seem to think you wouldn't mind.'

'I don't mind exactly,' Kate said slowly. The students were fourth-year medical students having their first exposure to paediatrics and anaesthetics and they were generally enthusiastic and lively and normally she enjoyed teaching them. But both theatre lists she'd agreed to cover the next day were heavily loaded and since the registrar who normally helped out had his own list as well, and since they'd be sharing their ODA and one senior house officer, she wouldn't have a lot of time spare for instructing on techniques or letting the students help. 'I'm just not sure I'll be able to give them a very good session. How many are there?'

'Just six,' Agnes said brightly, running a finger along the list pinned behind her on the wall. 'No, probably only five in his group tomorrow. They'll be all right, won't they? They're very good, this current lot. I'm sure they won't be any bother. They'll just want to watch.'

'That'll be fine.' Kate managed a smile. It wouldn't be fair to treat the students that way but she'd try and fit in some time to show them some practical things. At that stage of their training, even getting the chance to look at the vocal cords when she was intubating—putting the tube down her patients' throats into their lungs so she could ventilate and administer the anaesthetic gases directly into their lungs—was exciting.

'The Prof did seem sure you'd be happy to do it,' Agnes said confidently. 'Oh, almost forgot, I'm supposed to ask you about Monday as well. The Professor realised this morning that he's supposed to be on call Monday but he was hoping to still be on the Isle of Wight till Tuesday. He's taking the boat across, you see. It's supposed to be very good sailing weather this weekend. He was hoping you wouldn't mind stepping in for him on the roster.'

But Kate hesitated, remembering Mark's tight expression when she'd tried to get out of the weekend. At that moment her colleague seemed the greater evil than the Prof. 'I'm supposed to be spending the weekend in Wiltshire,' she responded lamely. 'Mark wants me to help him with his garden and I did promise.' And after all, she'd covered for the Prof over Christmas and Easter. And, now she thought about it,

August bank holiday the year before. She didn't mind, of course she didn't mind, but this would be her first public holiday off in more than a year. 'I'm sorry—'

But Agnes' sniff made her break off. 'I'm sure you are, Dr Lamb,' the manager countered stiffly. 'I'm sure you're very sorry. But that doesn't help me, does it? Nor your poor patients, I might add. I have no idea where the Professor is staying in Southampton. I have no way of getting hold of him to tell him to come back early. He did say you wouldn't mind—'

'OK, I don't mind,' Kate said quickly, feeling guilty that she'd even attempted to find an excuse. The Prof, nearing retirement, had a busy, active social life and it was reasonable for him to expect a little leeway in terms of his on-call responsibilities. And, given that she'd never objected to helping him out before, it wasn't surprising he'd taken her own willingness to do Monday for him for granted.

Mark would understand. She'd take her own car down to the cottage so as not to inconvenience him and she could still help him Saturday and Sunday. Since it seemed the boss had already left and couldn't be contacted, she could hardly walk out and leave no consultant anaesthetist on first-on-call duty for Monday. After all, their patients had to come first.

'Don't worry about Monday, Agnes. I'll cover it. You'll just need to let switchboard know so they understand the change.'

'Thank you, Dr Lamb.' Agnes' small smile was appeased. 'I was sure I could count on you.'

Mark, though, reacted vastly differently to her helpfulness in agreeing to stand in on Monday.

'The wily old rat,' he said angrily, when Kate popped her head into his anaesthetic room briefly between cases towards the end of the afternoon. 'You mean he just skipped out of town leaving Agnes to do the dirty work?'

'I'm sure he meant to ask me personally,' she said gingerly. 'I'm sorry, Mark. But it'll work out fine. I'll bring my car down so you won't need to drive me back to town Sunday night.'

But Mark didn't care about the inconvenience to him; it was the Professor and Agnes Coffee he was furious with. Kate might be too generous for her own good but the old man and the administrator had never been slow about taking advantage of that. It certainly wasn't the first time the Prof had dumped something like this on her on a public holiday but he was going to make sure it was the last. 'Where is he?' he demanded.

Kate looked uncertain. 'Southampton, I think.'

'A hotel?'

'I'm not sure.' She shook her head. 'On his boat, perhaps. Agnes said she didn't know how to contact him. But it doesn't matter, does it? I've already said I'll cover—'

'You're not covering.' Mark sent her a dismissive look and waved her out. 'We've already decided you're taking the weekend off. Leave it with me,' he ordered. Normally, he recognised, he'd have let it ride. Normally he wouldn't have intervened so directly in her battles, primarily because she wouldn't have let him, but until then he'd also felt a little that if she was silly enough to let herself be used, then so be it. But now she looked too tired for him to let it just happen again. Much more of the way she'd been lately, and she'd be making herself sick. 'I'll sort him out,' he said tightly.

'But—'

'Go!' In no mood for delicate, conversational side-stepping, he waved her away again more impatiently. 'Get lost, Kate. I've heard enough.'

That at least worked. After another brief hesitation and a worried look she let the door swing shut behind her.

He didn't have a chance to get hold of Agnes before the end of his list after six and by then, predictably, the administrator was long gone. Doctors and nurses might be expected to work unsociable shifts, but the same was rarely true of the hospital's administrative staff.

He tried the Prof's home but there was no answer so he got hold of Agnes' home telephone number from the hospital switchboard and called her after he'd finished seeing the last of his patients out of Recovery.

'Agnes?' The manager had answered after one ring. 'Mark Summers. I need Prof's number in Southampton.'

'Oh, Dr Summers, the Professor left strict instructions he wasn't to be contacted by anyone. You see he's entertaining quite a few friends this weekend. In fact I'm driving down myself so I can join him to sail to Cowes on Saturday—'

'Agnes, I'm not asking a favour,' Mark said tersely. 'I'm telling you, I need that number. Now you can give it to me nicely, or I can lodge an official complaint about administrative bullying of anaesthetic medical staff.'

'*Bullying?*' Agnes sounded taken aback. 'I have no idea what you're talking about.'

'Kate Lamb covering Monday for Prof,' he said briskly.

'Oh, Dr Summers, I simply explained to Dr Lamb that we were short-staffed on Monday because of the

Professor being away and I merely asked if she wouldn't mind—'

'The number, Agnes.' He didn't have time for this and he knew the way the anaesthetic department administration worked well enough to lack any sympathy for the woman.

All medical staff in the department were allocated regular on-call duties. If the Professor had applied for leave in the authorised way, then it would have been Agnes' job to employ and pay for a locum so his after-hours work would be covered. Lizzie's was fortunate enough to have been spared the dramatic budget cuts other London teaching hospitals had suffered over recent years, but still new incentives for administrative staff to cut spending had been installed widely. Agnes' salary, he knew, was bolstered annually by bonuses which rose as anaesthetic department spending dropped. Consequently, the less the department spent on locum medical and technical staff, the larger Agnes' bonus.

And he was confident Kate hadn't been offered locum-rate remuneration. He knew for a fact she hadn't been paid anything for the weeks of extra duties she'd done on the Professor's behalf over Christmas because he'd asked once whether she was doing the overtime for the money and her surprise had told him that she hadn't had any idea that she might have been entitled to any. Predictably, once he'd explained her rights, she'd refused to even consider lodging a back claim. She'd done the work for the sake of their patients, she'd told him firmly. She wasn't interested in earning extra money.

Even when he'd pointed out the money the department saved in locum fees only ended up in the administration staff bonuses at the end of the year and that she could—as most of them did these days—pay her extra earnings into one of the hospital's fund-raising efforts such as the one for the new bone-marrow transplant unit or the Christmas fund, she still hadn't felt right about lodging a claim for the earnings.

So, as was more likely, the boss was taking unauthorised—*paid*—leave, then Agnes was deliberately breaking standard procedure to both cover up for him and save the department money. In either case, Kate, the one weak link amongst all the anaesthetic staff, was being used.

'I want the number,' he repeated. 'And that complaint letter's going to be accompanied by a claim form for Dr Lamb's extra duties at Christmas and Easter for the past couple of years. By the way, how is it that the Prof seems to get far more annual leave than normal these days?'

'I wouldn't know anything about that, Dr Summers.' Agnes sounded riled now. 'It's really none of my business. Professor Carmody's number in Southampton, you were wanting, I think you said. Ah, here it is.' She read out a series of numbers crisply. 'I trust that will be all, Dr Summers.'

'Thank you, Agnes.' Mark smiled. 'You've been very helpful.'

'Naturally, with Professor Carmody's retirement next year, the position of Head of Department will become vacant,' Agnes added shrilly, her anger apparently renewed by what he thought had been a fairly pleasant sort of exchange. 'There has been some discussion about your own prospects of taking up that job, Dr Summers. Just a friendly word of warning, but I should take care, if I were you, not to offend either Professor Carmody or myself if you remain interested in that position.'

'A friendly word of warning to yourself, Agnes,' Mark countered briskly. He hadn't yet made up his mind whether he was prepared to take on the extra duties involved in being in charge of the department, but if he did choose to apply he'd been offered enough support from senior staff at both the hospital and college to suggest his prospects of securing the job were high. 'If I should decide to take up that position, you most certainly will be at the top of my list for review of your own job,' he said abruptly. 'And if I hear of you or Professor Carmody using Dr Lamb to cover your own deficiencies again, then that review will certainly be unfavourable. Am I making myself clear?'

'I think you're being very foolish, Dr Summers. I suspect you're relying on your reputation to protect you, but, I warn you, that's very unwise in these times of difficult changes. No consultant should consider him or herself indispensable.'

'I'll just have to take that risk,' Mark retorted pleasantly. 'Thank you, Agnes.'

CHAPTER THREE

KATE couldn't believe it when Mark told her casually the next day when they met as they were just about to go into Theatres that he'd heard she wouldn't be needed at Lizzie's on Monday after all. 'So who's doing the day on call?' she demanded, her eyes wide.

She and Mark were the only consultants on staff who weren't married with children. Her own single status and lack of family, along with the fact that she knew Mark was always wanting to get away to the cottage, were the reasons she invariably offered to cover for leave.

Her own father had died when she was very young and her mother had succumbed after a long illness to a rare form of cancer just before Kate's twenty-first birthday, and she had no brothers or sisters or close relatives, but if she had had she knew she would have wanted to spend holidays especially with them too. She couldn't believe any of the other anaesthetists on staff would have voluntarily sacrificed their bank holiday and the chance to spend time with their families.

'Prof's coming back Sunday night now,' Mark revealed calmly. 'He's going to do Monday himself.'

'But I thought he was going away with friends on his boat?'

Her colleague's shrug suggested he didn't think the issue was particularly important. 'He's definitely coming back.'

'Oh.' Kate was still surprised. In her experience, the Prof took every opportunity he could these days to get away from Lizzie's. 'Well, so we'll have an extra day to spend in your garden,' she said weakly.

'Mmm.' He'd opened the door, ready to leave her to her first case, but then he hesitated, his expression amused. 'You don't look like you're looking forward to it.'

'Oh…but I am,' she assured him wanly. 'Hugely.' She was, sort of, looking forward to a few days away, but a part of her was still a bit worried she might be driven screaming mad by his garden after the third day. She hadn't minded about coming back to be on call because at least that way, if the day hadn't turned out to be horribly busy, it would have given her a chance to either work on her research or make a less-enthusiastic start on the backlog of paperwork piling up in her office.

The Professor's students, the ones she'd agreed to have with her for her morning theatre session, arrived just after nine. One of the receptionists bleeped her to come and fetch them from outside Theatres because none of them seemed sure of where to go or what they should be doing.

Leaving her senior house officer to supervise her patient who was currently stable midway through her operation—she'd be less than a few seconds away if she was needed urgently—Kate skipped out of the theatre to greet the students, frowning slightly when she saw their nervous expressions.

'I thought you'd been attached to the Professor all week,' she said, puzzled by their apparent concern. 'Hasn't he brought you into Theatres every day?'

'He's just been giving us a lecture on anaesthetics for half an hour each morning then sending us away to the library to read about it,' one of them told her.

'He told us you'd be showing us all the practical stuff today.'

'Oh.' Kate blinked at that. Pity the Prof hadn't thought to warn her, she thought wanly. Of all days, today wasn't a good one for her to take a lot of time out for teaching. But then she could hardly blame the poor students for that. 'OK, then, blue smocks, tops and trousers for the boys and either the same for girls or the dresses, whatever you prefer. Cover your hair with paper hats, you girls with very long hair might find you need two, and choose spare theatre shoes out of the boxes in the dressing rooms,' she explained, pointing out where they needed to go. 'Leave all your valuables locked in the spare lockers including your watches and jewellery. Don't forget to pin your name badges to your tops so we know who you are.' She waved them along to the changing area. 'Come along and wait outside the anaesthetic room attached to Theatre Three when you're ready. You'll find masks in a box on the wall outside the theatre.'

But when they were all ready outside she saw half of them had their masks on backwards. 'On these ones, the green side is inside,' she instructed with a gentle smile, sympathising with their embarrassment because she remembered her own early embarrassing days as a student in theatres all too well. 'The way to tell, if you don't remember the colours or the way it's pleated, is that the word "inside" is printed in small print on that side.'

When she'd been a young medical student, her first contact with the secluded world of Theatres had come in her fourth year when she'd been attached to a very macho, male orthopaedic surgery team. The more senior doctors on the team—at that time she'd been a rather keen if disorganised and desperately anxious-to-please female who knew nothing about rugby or cricket—had regarded her with appalled bemusement.

She'd been very much thrown in at the deep end. She'd been ignored by everyone except the team's registrar—whose only intervention had been the odd surreptitious brush against her breasts or grope of her bottom whenever he'd thought he could get away with it—and nobody had taken the time to explain theatre protocols or dress or etiquette to her. She'd somehow blundered through the attachment but it hadn't been easy.

Thinking about her first day still made her blush now. She'd ventured into theatre for the first time to watch, and possibly, if she was very, very lucky, to be able to hold a retractor for one of her team's operations, only no one had told her about needing to change clothes. Her nervous arrival in normal street dress instead of theatre gear had sent the nursing staff into a screaming panic and had meant the entire list had had to be delayed while the theatre had been cleaned.

The team had never quite forgiven her for that. The other doctors had certainly never forgotten. She still saw the registrar from time to time, a consultant surgeon now at another London hospital, because he'd married one of her friends from medical school meaning they sometimes met socially. He invariably enjoyed reminding her of that day.

Just as he still invariably seemed to enjoy groping her, she acknowledged, her teeth gritting. Visiting Mary tended to be an uneasy experience because Kate could never be sure when her husband might attempt to press her into a corner somewhere and whisper obscene suggestions. Why such a successful, well-regarded man, married to such a lovely, wonderful woman with two beautiful children would ever—?

She would never, she acknowledged, shaking her head briefly, *never* understand men.

'OK, you're all fine now,' she said, once the students had their masks corrected. 'Now, I'll take you in. You'll find it hot inside, I'm afraid. Because we're dealing with children who lose heat so quickly, all our theatres are kept very warm and we use warming mattresses and radiant heaters as well until the drapes are on our patients, plus all the fluids are warmed and the gases are warmed and humidified. If you start to feel uncomfortable or faint, just come out here again for a few minutes where it's cooler. Don't be embarrassed about it, it takes time to get used to working in heat and nobody will mind if you have to leave. Mr Webb is operating. Our patient is a little girl who's having her right kidney removed because of a Wilms' tumour. If you remember, that's a type of cancer that's quite common in children. Remember, if he invites you to come closer to look at what he's doing, you mustn't touch any of the cloth guards around the patient. Everything green is sterile and take care not to let any part of you or your clothes brush against any of the surgeons or nurses.'

She'd already explained before she'd left about the students coming and the theatre staff were prepared for them. 'Come on in,' the surgeon invited, his eyes twinkling above his masks as he motioned them forward. 'We're going well, Kate. We'll be closing within twenty minutes.'

'Thanks, Bill.' Kate moved to take over again from the junior doctor who'd been supervising the anaesthetic for her. 'No problems?'

'Very peaceful,' the younger doctor whispered,

while the surgeon began telling the students what they'd been doing. The other doctor showed Kate the anaesthetic record where he'd been making regular recordings of the child's heart rate, blood pressure, oxygen levels and pupil size, linking the measurements together to form a serial chart. 'No signs of any distress and her blood pressure and urine output have both been great.'

'Well done.' Kate checked the machine connected to Sarah's ear which was recording the amount of oxygen in her blood, noting that the measure was entirely normal, then, by routine, used the stethoscope she'd taped in place over the left side of her breastbone earlier to check her heart sounds and that they were still ventilating both sides of their patient's lungs equally. Because the surgeon had made his incision across the uppermost part of the child's abdomen, at the level of her lower ribs, access to her chest wasn't ideal, but everything sounded normal.

'Wilms' tumours are a relatively common tumour of childhood,' the surgeon was saying as he worked. 'This little girl was lucky enough to have had hers discovered early. She'd had no symptoms but she fell down some steps last week and banged her head and her hip and the injury made the blood vessels inside her tumour start to haemorrhage. That made the cancer swell up quickly and gave her some pain. The GP her parents took her to to have the cut on her head stitched noticed the mass. He sent her straight to us and we made the diagnosis by CT scan.'

'Will this cure her?' one of the students asked, eyeing the kidney and the greyish area of tumour the surgeon had already removed.

'Hopefully,' the surgeon told him. 'We use chemotherapy as well, aimed at killing any cells which

may have already spread, and sometimes radiotherapy
for discreet masses, depending on the pathology and
what the oncologists here decide. Commonly this
tumour spreads either directly to the structures nearby
or to the lungs. There's no sign of spread here and
the lungs on scanning at least are clear. The prognosis
mostly depends on the grade of tumour. Once the
pathologists have a look at this under the microscope
we'll know more. Survival figures are pretty good
these days for Wilms' tumours. When I was a child
tumours like this were virtually universally fatal but
here at Lizzie's these days we're seeing about ninety-
five per cent five-year survival across the board.
That's about right, wouldn't you say, Kate?'

'Ninety to ninety-five,' Kate agreed, nodding. 'As
you say, dependent on the type of tumour. Sarah here
is in a good prognostic group. There's every reason
to expect she'll be completely cured.'

Shortly afterwards the surgeon left his registrar to
finish closing the wound while he took the students
across to the X-ray board on the wall of the theatre
to take them through the child's pre-op scans.

By the time the younger surgeon had Sarah's main
wound closed and covered and her drains sutured into
place and firmly fastened, Kate had reversed the muscle relaxant she'd been using to keep the child's
tummy relaxed and switched off the main gas she'd
been using to keep Sarah asleep. She gently lowered
the concentration of nitrous oxide she'd been using to
bring her around. Kate bent quietly over her, continuing the oxygen by mask and bag and murmuring
gentle words while she woke.

As soon as she felt resistance against the ET tube,
the tube between Sarah's mouth and lungs, she
smoothly suctioned and withdrew it. 'Good girl,

Sarah,' she murmured, when the child muttered something unintelligible. 'Good girl. I'm taking you through to the wake-up room to see Mummy and Daddy now. Your operation's finished.'

The students were still busy with Bill, questioning him in enthusiastic depth about the X-rays and scans, so she left them there and went with Sarah into Recovery.

'She's had fentanyl and an antiemetic at eight-forty,' she told the receiving recovery nurse, referring to the pain relief and anti-vomiting agent she'd administered while the nurse quickly connected the oxygen and pumps to the recovery supply. 'We'll keep her on a continuous pump for at least twenty-four hours.' Kate examined Sarah again then ran briskly through the intravenous fluid regime she'd charted and the observations she wanted of vital signs and urine output. 'I've given her three hundred mils of blood so far but let me know if you get a lot more in the drains.'

'No problem.' Siobhan, the nurse, had Sarah's teddy ready and she slid it in beside her, and Kate smiled as the drowsy child's hand promptly closed around it. She nodded for her anxious-looking parents, who until then had been hovering by the door in their theatre gear, to come forward.

'Everything went fine,' she told them reassuringly. 'Mr Webb is just talking to some medical students now but he'll be in in a few minutes to talk to you about her. But everything looked good inside and the tumour wasn't difficult to remove. He seems very happy.'

Their next case was a little boy with the same, although much larger, sort of tumour as Sarah's. When Kate had met with the family on the ward that morning it had been obvious that Thomas's parents were far more anxious about his surgery than he was himself, so between them all they'd agreed that they wouldn't come into the anaesthetic room with him.

Instead they hovered outside in the corridor, peering in through the round windows of the anaesthetic room doors, and Kate took care to keep her most reassuring expression fixed in place.

She was always happy to have parents present in the anaesthetic room but in her experience if they were very upset that only served to increase the child's alarm and, given that her sole concern now was for her patient, she'd been glad they'd seen the sense of staying outside.

Thomas was drowsy from his premed and he looked calm. 'I'm having an operation,' he told her huskily, his big dark eyes staring up at her trustingly as she inserted a tiny cannular into the blood vessel she'd anaesthetised earlier with EMLA cream. 'I'm going to be sleeping the whole time and I'm not going to wake up until the doctor's finished.'

'That's right,' Kate said softly. When he'd arrived in the room she'd gently put a clear oxygen mask over his face to build up his oxygen levels before she intubated him and now she slowly began pushing the contents of the syringe she'd prepared into his new cannular. 'You're a good boy. Can you count to ten for me, Thomas?'

'One,' he whispered obediently, long dark lashes coming down to conceal his eyes. 'Two...'

As soon as he was asleep and intubated she nodded towards the window to his parents, and the nurse who'd been waiting with them, explaining what they'd been seeing, steered them away to where they'd wait in the relatives' room attached to Theatres until it was time to come back to see their son in Recovery.

Thomas's surgery went well. Once again, despite being bigger, the tumour resection proved relatively uncomplicated and Bill was fairly confident there'd been no spillage of cells from the yellow tumour-mass during the delicate removal process. There were no obvious signs of spread outside the kidney and when Kate woke Thomas afterwards behind his oxygen mask, he even managed a little smile for her.

Having the students with her for the rest of the day slowed Kate slightly, but not too much. She went with them to buy lunch between lists and they brought the food back and ate in a spare staff room, using the half-hour to review what they'd seen that morning before beginning on their new list, with Giles the surgeon this time, after lunch.

Just after four the last case for the day was brought into Theatres. A tiny baby who'd been born prematurely the day before, the contents of her little abdomen were protruding through a gap in her tummy where the skin and muscle hadn't closed properly just to the right of her tummy button. Giles had squeezed her onto the end of his list as an emergency case.

As she wheeled the anaesthetised baby through for the operation, Kate glanced towards the students waiting clustered along the theatre, sure they must be tired by now from their long day. 'You've seen a lot today,' she told them. 'You've worked hard.' In the latter cases, where the children had been older and relaxed about having observers, she'd even let them help with intubating and bagging and they'd done a good job. 'I'm happy for you to leave now, if you like.'

But they asked instead if they could stay and they were clearly fascinated by the baby's condition.

'Not uncommon,' Giles told them, when they questioned him about it. 'We've got a biased sample here because we take babies from all over the country, of course, but this little one would be the third one we've seen in the last month or so. Agreed, Kate?'

'Probably the last two months,' Kate amended, nodding for the radiant heater above the table to be switched off now that Giles and his registrar had begun the operation. The theatre was heated up to twenty-nine degrees and the baby was lying on sheets above a heated blanket, and Giles had covered her abdominal contents with warmed, sterile and damp swabs, then covered those with plastic.

Heat as well as fluid loss were potential problems Kate had to manage in all surgery on premature babies, but here, with so much bowel exposed, the risks were magnified. She had a rectal thermometer in place as well as all her usual monitoring devices plus a bladder catheter, a central line into a vein in the baby's neck providing a measure of her fluid levels and a tube going from the baby's nose to her stomach so she could remove extra fluid and gas from the bowel to help Giles fit the contents back inside the tummy.

Giles enlarged the hole in the abdominal wall and stretched it with his fingers, explaining to the students as he worked exactly what he was doing. 'And now,' he said cheerfully, sending an enquiring look towards Kate as the surgical registrar tented the edges of the wound for him, 'we see just how much we can fit in. This bit is up to Dr Lamb,' he told them. 'Only Dr Lamb can tell us when we've stretched the abdomen enough to compromise baby's breathing. Even if I can squeeze everything back in first time, we don't achieve anything if the poor baby's so squashed by it all she can't ever breathe again.'

As always Kate hoped that all would go well first time, but this time it became obvious fairly quickly that it wouldn't. 'Too tight,' she warned Giles after a few moments, when it became obvious that the pressure in the baby's abdomen was increasing too much for normal breathing. She explained to the students about how she was monitoring the oxygen levels in their patient's blood along with the level of pressure she was needing to inflate her little lungs. 'We're going to have to do this in stages, sorry, Giles.'

'I expected it,' Giles told her brightly, withdrawing some of the bowel he'd replaced. He encased the loops of bowel that would have to stay outside in sterile mesh, then sutured the edges of the mesh to the tissue inside the edges of the wound, talking the technique through for the fascinated students. 'Over the next few days Terence and I will gradually squeeze off the end of the mesh and push a little bit more of bowel each time into the tummy,' he told them, exchanging looks with his registrar. 'A bit like squeezing toothpaste out of a tube, only this time the end of the tube is the inside of the tummy. When it's all back inside finally we'll bring her back here to Theatres and take away the mesh and close her up. The whole thing will take about a week to ten days maximum. She'll always have a bit of a scar here, of course, but hopefully we'll be able to minimise that and in time it'll fade.'

'We'll have to give her nourishment intravenously for a couple of weeks,' Kate explained. 'Obviously her bowel won't start working properly until it's recovered from all of this handling.'

'It's incredible,' one of the students breathed, and they were all watching intently as Giles finished fastening the edges of the mesh tube in place and began wrapping it in dressings to protect it.

'It's really all very simple,' Giles said happily. 'When it goes well. Just about finished here, Kate.'

Kate nodded, preparing to reverse the anaesthetic. The baby would go back to the neonatal unit that night and she'd remain there until after her wound was finally closed.

The students came with Kate for the transfer to Neonates, then came back to Theatres to change into their normal clothes. 'Professor Carmody will be back next week so he'll be looking after you all again,' she told them. 'But if you keep in touch with me I'll let you know when we're going to be closing our last little baby's tummy and I'm sure Giles won't mind if you come along that day with me to see the operation.'

They were obviously enthusiastic about that, but the exchange of looks her announcement about the Prof being back had provoked warned Kate that none of them was particularly excited about the prospect of returning to his teaching. She made a mental note to have a word to the Prof about them. He'd probably forgotten how exciting theatre could be for students, she realised. Instilling theory was important, of course, and clearly he'd been trying to do that, but she'd tell him how much they seemed to have enjoyed their time seeing theory being put into practice today.

Mark put his head into Kate's anaesthetic room shortly after and caught her standing still, for once, an introspective look on her face. 'What's up?'

She jumped slightly, as if his words startled her. 'I

had some students with me today,' she said huskily. 'I was just thinking about them.'

'About how terrible young people are these days?' he teased. 'About how when we were young we used to work twenty-eight hours a day and walk, nay, run—run at a gallop—eighteen miles home just to fetch our pencils?'

She laughed. 'Not at all, they were great,' she said lightly. 'Very enthusiastic. Actually, I was a bit worried about their training. They've been doing an anaesthetic attachment for two weeks now with Prof and today was the first time they've been in Theatre.'

Mark frowned. 'What's he been doing with them?'

'Lecturing them for half an hour,' she revealed. 'It's such a shame because they're a really keen bunch. They never stopped questioning Bill and Giles while they were operating. They could have seen loads in these last weeks. I thought perhaps I might have a word with him—'

'Leave it to me.' Mark spoke swiftly. 'I've been meaning to talk to him about the students for a while.' The less contact, he'd decided, between the Prof and Kate in future, the better. After their frank discussion the night before the older man should know better than to overtly lump his work onto Kate, but Mark still wouldn't put it past the old fool to risk a more subtle approach.

'The sooner his retirement comes, the better,' he added grimly. 'Those poor kids. This is their careers he's playing with. The more they see, the better at this stage. Another few years and they won't be watching this they'll be having to do it.'

'I'm sure he thinks he's doing his best,' Kate said appeasingly, but Mark was equally sure she was wrong. The old man had lost whatever enthusiasm

he'd once had for the job. His only interests these
days were his boat, his whisky and Agnes Coffee, and
it was time he was gone.

'Are you finished?' He looked around. She was
alone in the anaesthetic room and the nurses looked
as if they were almost through clearing up the theatre.
He knew her list was over because he'd seen Giles,
the surgeon she'd been working with, on his way to
the changing rooms ten minutes before, just after his
own list had finished.

It was Friday and he was keen to get down to the
cottage. He'd told her that he'd collect her from her
flat at six although, knowing Kate, he'd always
known it would end up being much later. But, still,
the sooner she could be ready, the better. 'Want a lift
home to get your things?'

'I just want to run up and check on a couple of the
children from Bill's list this morning,' she said huskily. 'We had two little kids with kidney resections
for Wilms' tumours and I want to make sure they're
all right before I leave for the weekend. That'll take
me about twenty minutes and then I've just got a few
other things to tidy up.' She frowned up at the clock.
'I could be home by seven, seven-thirty at the latest.
You go now, Mark. I can walk home. How about you
come around about eight?'

'Seven-thirty,' he insisted. If he gave her more time
she'd only dawdle around the hospital and find more
work for herself. 'Tim's on call tonight and for the
weekend so you can relax. You're leaving everyone
in good hands.'

He'd insisted, but he hadn't really thought she'd be
ready for him. Consequently he wasn't at all surprised
to find her in a state of disorganised panic when she
opened her front door to him. 'Ten minutes,' she

cried, running ahead of him up the stairs. 'I've just got home. I want to take a quick shower, then all I have to do is throw some clothes into a bag. Turn on the TV, if you like. There might be some news on somewhere.'

But Mark didn't like. Instead he occupied himself for the fifteen minutes until she appeared again by prowling around her little flat, every now and then lifting up one of the anaesthetic texts or journals—as far as he could see her sole reading matter—doing his best to distract himself from the sound of the water and tuneless humming coming from the bathroom door she'd left happily ajar just through the other side of flat's lone bedroom.

He'd been there loads of times before. Not for a while now, he conceded, which was perhaps part of the reason he'd forgotten how dour and poky the place was.

The main staff quarters at Lizzie's were actually quite pleasant but Kate had been given this place in the secondary annexe—a building generally used only short term for overflow when the main building was full—and for vague reasons of her own, such as not having time and being happy where she was, had never bothered moving over to the other building when space had become available.

'You should buy a place of your own,' he shouted, when the water shut off. 'You must be able to afford it by now, can't you?'

'I could probably afford it,' she shouted back. 'But do I really want my own place? I don't know if I do. I'm hardly here as it is.'

'You can't live in hospital flats all your life.'

'It's not that bad.' She peered out at him through the broad gap of the open door. Busy fastening a bath towel above her breasts, she was so completely un-selfconscious that he knew then, with absolute certainty, that her awareness of him as a man who might, perchance, take even a passing interest in the shape of her body beneath the towel was non-existent.

'It's liveable,' she added, looking around the walls of the tiny flat with apparent cheerfulness. 'And it's so close to the hospital.'

'Too close,' he growled, turning away from her abruptly. 'Too bloody close. At least you should move over to the main block. How much do they charge you for this dump?'

'It comes out of my salary.' He heard sounds of her moving about in her bedroom. 'I never take much notice of how much it is. And I like it here better than the main block. It might not be as nice but it's definitely quieter. And at least there're no hassles with it. I never have to worry about rates or maintenance or anything like that.'

'Doesn't look like anyone worries about mainte-nance,' he muttered, frowning at the dark stains on the gas water-heating unit above the sink in the tiny corner of the room that passed for a kitchen. 'Have you had the boiler checked lately?'

'Stop fussing.' Dressed now in jeans that clung lovingly to the curve of her thighs and a loose-fit pale blue blouse, she emerged from her room smiling. 'It's fine. Everything's fine.' With her blonde, silky hair free about her shoulders she looked, he thought, about eighteen, but now she twisted it up into a knot at the back of her head and pinned it, restoring her appearance to something more familiar. 'The only tiny little complaint I've got is that they don't turn this particular building's heating off until July. They're predicting a hot summer this year. None of the windows open properly so the place will probably be sweltering from next month.'

'You shouldn't be here with this thing if the windows aren't open,' he said grimly, eyeing the boiler. 'I don't like you living here, Kate. You should be somewhere better.'

'I'm perfectly happy.' Increasing his frustration, she seemed to find his irritation amusing. 'Relax,' she chided. 'It's not that bad. Now, do you want coffee or are you ready to go?'

'We're going.' He felt a sudden, urgent need to be out of the ghastly place. He collected the small knapsack she'd assembled, but she collected her other bag before he could reach it and he stood back and waited for her to open the door. 'You haven't even got decent locks,' he observed disparagingly. 'Any kid could break in here.'

'In three years no one's even tried,' she said, locking the door behind them.

'Three years?' He stared at her, appalled by how long she'd been living there. 'Has it really been three years?'

'Just about.' She pulled a face when she saw his expression. 'Stop it,' she ordered calmly. 'Stop being so critical. I like it here.'

'It's time, Kate,' he said quietly, vowing to overcome her arguments and find an estate agent for her first thing the following week, 'for a radical change in your lifestyle.'

CHAPTER FOUR

THEY stopped at a pub in Marlborough for a meal and a drink and it was dark by the time Mark turned off the road onto the rutted farm track leading up to the cottage. He sent Kate a sideways smile, then opened the doors and went to collect their things, stilling when he registered the weight in her second bag as he lifted it from the boot of the car.

'Kate,' he growled.

'It's only a few journals and a couple of new textbooks. Just some stuff I need to read.' She wrinkled her nose at him but her green eyes sparked defensively in the light spilling from her open door. 'Mark, you can't really expect me to go cold turkey.'

'But cold turkey is exactly,' he told her tersely, 'what I do expect.' Ignoring her wail of protest, he dropped the bag back into the car, slammed the boot shut on it, and slid the keys into the side pocket in his jeans. 'If you're desperate to read something, you'll find plenty of books inside.'

'Novels,' she said disparagingly, as if scornful of the self-indulgence signalled by ownership of such objects.

Mark, at the end of the meandering paved path that led to the main door of the cottage, unlocked the door and switched on the outside light, then turned around, frowning at her while he waited for her to catch up. 'You've given up reading?'

'These days I only have time to read useful things.'

He shook his head slowly, shocked by that. The

thought that she'd spent the last three years living in that miserable flat without even the joy of the fiction she'd once enjoyed to distract her from the demands of work appalled him. 'Do you still go to the gym?'

'The gym?' She looked guilty, although he didn't know why since when they'd been registrars together she'd always made time for the aerobics sessions she loved. 'I haven't been to a class in…well, probably in two years,' she said lamely. 'I keep telling myself I should make time, for my health's sake if nothing else, but I'm usually too exhausted by the time I get home these days. Most nights I just cook myself up some soup then fall into bed.'

'Oh, Kate.' Mark just stared at her, stricken, abruptly, with mute guilt. He should have taken more time himself, he knew. He saw her a lot at work but he should have taken more time these past two years particularly to make sure she was OK. His own life was busy too but he was still supposed to be her friend. Clearly lately he hadn't been much of one. 'Look, perhaps you should consider cutting out a couple of sessions—'

'What are you talking about?' With an impatient look, she pushed past him into the cottage. 'Silly man,' she chided. 'I'm fine. I know I've probably taken on a little bit much this year but I'm very happy with my life.' She looked around the entrance way then wandered into the main living room, her eyes widening. 'Oh, you've done heaps.'

'There's still some to do.' Electing to leave any discussion about her work, for now at least, Mark followed her slowly. The cottage, when he'd bought it, had been neglected for many years and abandoned, but gradually, using his own labour and with the help of a couple of enthusiastic local tradesmen for guidance, he was restoring it in a way designed to be sympathetic to its era but in line with his own, more modern needs as well. Originally the design had been very closed in, but he'd taken out one wall to open it up more, bringing light and space into the rooms, and both the plumbing and electrical systems had been completely upgraded. 'I'm hoping to have it finished by Christmas.'

'Oh, it's lovely.' She walked through into the stone-floored kitchen and eating area. 'I love it. And there's a courtyard.'

'The flagstones are original,' he explained, pleased with her enjoyment. It was a relatively mild night, and he opened the broad doors leading out onto it and turned on the outside lights so she could see the stones properly. His sister had planted huge clay pots with flowers and herbs, decorating the space, and the grapevine wound around the trellis above had grown leafier since his last visit. 'They'd been covered with cement. It took about six months to clean it all off.'

'It's wonderful.' She laughed her delight. 'I can't believe you've done all this. It's amazing. I remember this place as practically a ruin. Mark, you're a genius.'

'It's been fun.' He caught a baby, fluttering moth that must have been attracted by the lights, closed his palm around it, then released it outside again. 'Hard work, but fun. What would you like? Coffee? Wine?'

'Tea, please.' She'd bent to inhale the fragrance from one of the flowerpots and she turned around with a smile. 'It's too late for me for wine and if I have coffee at this hour I'll be awake all night.'

He put water on, then carried their bags through to their respective bedrooms. When the drinks were ready he took them, along with a soft blanket, out to where she sat on one of the wrought-iron benches in the courtyard.

'It's not summer yet,' he reminded her, passing her the blanket before her tea, then taking one of the other benches for himself. 'There's still some chill in the air.'

'Thanks.' She tucked the blanket around her shoulders, then stared up at the sky, smiling, while she stirred her tea. 'The stars are gorgeous. They're never this clear in London. I think I understand now why you're always dashing away for your weekends. It must be wonderful having this here to escape to. I suppose you bring all your girlfriends down here for romantic weekends.'

Mark felt his mouth twitch. '*All* my girlfriends,' he mocked. 'That's a rather alarming way of putting it. How many do you imagine I have, Kate?'

'Oh, heaps.' She waved an airy hand in the air. 'Dozens? I don't know. Am I close?'

'No.' He didn't elaborate. 'What about you and boyfriends?'

'Are you for real?' Her startled laugh was light and tinkling in the still evening air. 'Me? Boyfriends? With the hours I work these days? Oh, Mark, you're not serious, are you? You know me better than that. Who would put up with me?'

'Well, there was Simon Brent,' he reminded her. He knew for certain she'd gone out with that particular surgeon for several months at least because Simon had been cut up enough about it when it had ended to cry drunkenly on his shoulder one night. 'And Peter Webster—'

'Simon was two years ago and Peter Webster asked me out twice ages ago and I thought we seemed to get on OK, but he never asked me again,' she said brightly. 'I don't know what I did to put him off but as far as I can tell the poor man's still avoiding me.'

He smiled. 'You're not fooling me, Kate.' She was a beautiful woman. Her dedication and the way her mind worked might be too much of a challenge for most, but the rest of her was exquisite. Even if she spent every hour of the day at Lizzie's, he refused to believe that the rest of the male staff in the place hadn't at least been tempted by the body. 'I don't believe you never get asked out.'

'I get the odd approach,' she admitted lightly. 'But honestly, Mark. I don't have time for dating even if I was interested. It all seems so pointless to me these days. Frankly, I don't need the stress. I'd really just rather be working.'

'What stress?' He finished his coffee, then slid his cup away and stretched his legs out, tilting his head to study her. 'You find going out and having fun stressful? Most people find that sort of thing a way of relieving stress from work.'

She dropped her eyes. 'Well, perhaps I'm different to other people.'

'You're different, all right.' But he regarded her fondly. 'Kate, you know, you've got to make some changes in your life, sweet pea. You're going to end up burnt out and sick in a few years if you keep going at this rate. You need to learn how to relax again. You have to get a proper life for yourself outside of work.'

'But I love my work, Mark.' She still sounded bright but he sensed his refusal to acknowledge her words was beginning to aggravate her. 'I love what I do. My work is my life. I wouldn't want it to be any other way.'

'I love my work too,' he said gently. 'And I think

I'm better at what I do because I let myself have a life too.'

'It's different for you,' she argued. 'You were shocked into changing when perhaps you really didn't need to. You know you used to be the same as me and you loved it that way too. I truly believe that if your father hadn't died when he did you'd probably still be spending just as much time at Lizzie's as I—' She broke off suddenly, her expression turning stricken. 'Damn!' she exclaimed huskily. 'I didn't mean to say that. I'm sorry, Mark. I shouldn't have—'

'It's all right.' He held up his hand, neither wanting nor needing her apology. 'I don't mind,' he said firmly. In quiet moments he still, of course, grieved for his father, but the hard edge of grief, the hard, piercing pain of loss was blunted now and, although he still bore some guilt that his father hadn't felt able to turn to him when he had most needed support, most of his memories were good ones.

'And, you know, you're right,' he conceded. He had once lived his life around his work—never, he thought, to the extreme that Kate seemed to now, but much more so than was healthy. But his father's sudden suicide had been brought on, the inquest had decided, by depression stemming from the stress of his heavy workload as a general practitioner in sole practice.

In his grief, and also to appease his mother who had seemed suddenly terrified that the same fate might befall her only son, he'd confronted the way he was living his own life and made changes designed to protect his own psyche.

He'd bought the cottage with vague ideas of it lessening his mother's fears as well as protecting himself from a similar fate to his father. He'd rationalised that the—at that stage still undetectable—stress of the busy career job he loved would always be diluted by being able to escape to this peaceful retreat.

'Since I bought the cottage, though, I've come to realise that I didn't need to,' he said quietly. 'I'm not the way Dad was. We're different sorts of personalities. He was an intensely private person. He didn't discuss his work even with Mum. He would have found it intolerable to admit he wasn't coping. I'm more rational. If I felt I wasn't coping I wouldn't have any qualms about walking away. But still I don't regret this. It's my hobby now.'

'I'm glad you see that,' she said softly. 'About you being different to your father, I mean. Because you are incredibly different, Mark. I only met your father once but he seemed very much the stereotyped stalwart, devoted lone GP type. You've always been much more relaxed. I never thought for a second that you could ever—' She broke off. 'Well,' she finished gently. 'You know.'

'What about you?'

She looked startled. 'Me? What? *Depression,* you mean?'

'Why not?' He lifted one shoulder, watching her carefully. 'The way you're going these days, I'd consider you at risk.'

'But that's ridiculous.' She put down her tea. 'Mark, look at me.' She lifted up her arms. 'I'm happy as anything. I'm not remotely depressed.'

Perhaps not yet, but he worried about her future. 'Getting away from Lizzie's has still been good for me in terms of getting my sense of perspective back,' he told her quietly. 'It is only work. It might be fantastic, challenging, satisfying work, but at the end of the day it's only work. In reality, if we weren't there for the kids, someone else would be, doing exactly the same things in exactly the same ways.'

'I know that,' she insisted. 'But I want it to be me doing those things.'

'Are you able to think of anything but that at the moment? Have you even thought about your future? Have you given any thought at all to marriage, or having children of your own?'

'Marriage?' She'd been part way through refilling her tea from the pot, but now she dumped the pot down with a thump. 'Oh, Mark.' She looked appalled. 'Can you imagine me married?'

Her comment puzzled him. 'Why not?'

'Because I'm—' But she broke off again, seeming bemused. 'Well, I just don't think so,' she finished hastily.

'But you love children.'

'Of course I do, that's why I work with them, but that doesn't mean I have to have my own,' she said lightly. 'I really don't see that I'm ever going to have the time to have my own. Honestly, I think my maternal impulses will be quite satisfied if I just keep working at Lizzie's the rest of my life. I think of my patients as my children.'

While he was still trying to work out how to answer that, she quickly drained her tea, put the blanket aside, and came and looped her arms round his neck, enveloping him briefly in the warm, heady fragrance of her scent. 'Enough heavy stuff,' she murmured. 'I'm tired and I'm going to bed.' She pressed her mouth briefly to his cheek, then dropped her arms. 'And you must be tired too from all that driving, so don't stay up too late. I'll see you tomorrow. Am I in the same room as usual?'

'At the end of the hall,' he said quietly, not moving. ''Night, Katie.'

'*Kate,*' she corrected, on her way out. 'You know I hate Katie.'

Kate slept wonderfully. She couldn't remember the last time she'd slept so soundly and without waking. Normally at the flat she fell into a heavy sleep quickly only to wake up several times before finally waking irreversibly around dawn. This morning, when she finally sat up against her pillows, her watch on the little lace-covered table by the bed where she'd left it the night before told her it was almost nine.

'That bed is unbelievably comfortable,' she told Mark, padding out, still in her pyjamas and bare feet, to where he was sitting in the courtyard in the sun, the morning newspaper spread before him evidence that he'd been up long enough himself to have driven quite a way to buy it. 'At least that's my excuse for being so lazy. Hi.'

'Hi.' He smiled at her. 'The coffee in the plunger's fresh and there're pastries in the bag on the table.' He turned a page of his paper. 'You can bring me one too while you're up.'

'Pastries?' She went to find them. 'Yummy.' He'd brought several custard and fruit ones along with a couple of *pain-au-chocolat* type ones and two little fruit tarts. 'Are these all for us or are you expecting a bus-load to arrive?'

'I didn't know what you'd prefer.' He gave her an easy grin as she plonked the bag and two plates she'd found in one of his very tidy cupboards in the middle of the table outside. 'There's bacon and a dozen eggs in the fridge if you'd prefer.'

'Tomorrow,' she vowed, coming back outside with

the coffee. It was a long time since she'd had a cooked breakfast. Normally she satisfied herself with a few mouthfuls of coffee and a couple of slices of bread and Marmite. Her last proper breakfast was probably, she reflected, the last time she'd been here. 'What a beautiful day.' The flagstones were cool beneath her feet but the morning sun was blissfully warm on her back. 'Perfect for gardening. Lucky I thought to bring sun cream.' Mark had smooth, even skin and tanned easily without burning but she was so pale at the moment that even now in the spring she'd probably burn in an hour.

'About the gardening,' he said sedately. 'There isn't any.'

'What?' She blinked at him. 'Yes, there is.' She gestured vaguely out to the thick, tangled collection of greenery and flowers she could see off to the left. 'What's that, then?'

He smiled. 'I didn't mean there isn't a garden, Kate,' he said, with exaggerated patience. 'I mean there isn't any gardening to do.'

'But that's why I'm here.'

'Jilly keeps it pretty much under control,' he said smoothly. 'In fact she'll probably turn all territorial if we even pluck a weed. It's become a bit of a hobby for her.'

'A hobby? Jilly?' Licking her fingers free of the syrup they'd picked up from the pastries, Kate wandered across to the bricked wall around the courtyard and looked out into what she'd assumed was a jungle but what she could now see, with the benefit of her memory of his sister's own magnificently disordered garden, was a beautifully chaotic wildflower-studded and scented English garden. 'You…con man, Mark Summers,' she accused weakly. 'I came down here because I thought you needed me. You had me thinking I'd be hauling topsoil all weekend.'

'I may have misled you,' he drawled.

'There's no *may* about it,' she grumbled, meandering back to the table and fixing him with a soulful look. 'But I expect I'll forgive you.'

'I'm relieved. I didn't know anyone still wore pyjamas.' His expression mocking, he reached out and tugged at the sleeve of her top as she took her seat again. 'Where are these from?'

'John Lewis,' she said brightly. 'In Oxford Street. About four years ago. They're very comfortable.'

'I'm sure they are,' he said evenly, but he didn't look any more impressed.

Kate, not at all offended, since, knowing Mark as she did, the women he normally breakfasted with probably wore sexy negligees, merely wrinkled her nose at him. 'I got them in the boys' department, actually,' she confided, munching her way through a peach-impregnated custardy pastry. 'They had just what I was looking for. I had to sew up the flies by hand since I didn't have a machine but they've lasted well. I bought three pairs and they've still got years of wear in them.'

'Oh, Kate.' He shook his head as if mystified by her. 'You crazy woman.'

'I'm not crazy.' She laughed. 'They're sensible. And they were a very good buy—'

'You've got icing on your face.' He brushed her cheek and the corner of her mouth with his fingers. 'You have lovely skin. Very soft.'

'Thank you.' But she blinked up at him, bemused as much by the compliment as by the warm flush his unexpected touch seemed to have provoked. 'My face has been awful lately but I rubbed some of my new body lotion in last night so perhaps it's doing the trick?'

'Perhaps.' He looked back at his newspaper. 'I thought we might go for a walk around the stones at Avebury later. We could have lunch there. What do you think?'

'Sounds nice,' she agreed.

'Do you want some of this?'

'No, I'll just listen to the birds.' She didn't want to read newspapers. Leaning back in her chair, holding her coffee, she closed her eyes, enjoying the busy, morning hum of the insects and birds around them. The cottage was on an isolated part of the farm, several hundred yards from the nearest other house, and the peace and the scent of the garden were glorious. 'I haven't seen Jilly in ages,' she murmured. 'What's she doing these days?'

'She's going to try and call in over the weekend.' Kate remembered his sister and her family lived not too far away. 'So you can ask her yourself. I told her you might be coming down so she'll want to say hello.'

In the end they didn't go straight into Avebury because Mark, ignoring her complaints about her lack of fitness and sore legs, brutally forced her on a steep walk up what felt like a horrendous hill to get a close up view of one of Wiltshire's famous white horses. A huge figure carved into the chalky side of the hill, the horse could be seen from all around and personally, Kate decided, she'd have been just as happy seeing it from the road below.

'Stop grumbling,' he chided, not even breathless when they reached the top. 'The exercise is good for you.'

'It's killing me,' she protested, only half joking.

The climb hadn't been particularly high but she hadn't found it easy. 'My heart's beating like crazy. You're going to give me a heart attack.'

'You're too young.' He didn't seem remotely perturbed. 'Shut up and enjoy the view. Isn't it worth it?'

'Perhaps,' she gulped, looking around at the rolling green farmland. 'I really am going to have to try and…get back to the gym.'

'I'm surprised you're not fitter.' He eyed her assessingly. 'All the running around you do at work, I wouldn't have thought a little hill would bother you.'

'Same here.' She was exaggerating, a little, how difficult she'd found the climb. But only a little. And in truth she was shocked by finding herself in such a poor state of fitness. She did run about a lot at Lizzie's. And, considering the theatres were on the top floor and she invariably used the stairs rather than wasting time waiting for the lifts, she did get a lot of exercise. But obviously not enough.

'I'm sorry. I didn't mean to sound so unappreciative.' She put her arm around Mark's middle and hugged herself into his side briefly. 'It's sweet of you to bring me up here and I do love the view. Honestly. It's beautiful.'

'Good.' He smiled down at her but then, to her surprise, his eyes turned serious and he lowered his head abruptly and kissed her.

It wasn't an intrusive kiss, or even a particularly long one, it was merely gentle and quiet and not in the least bit unpleasant, but when he lifted his head again she blinked up at him, utterly astounded. 'What was that for?' she demanded rawly.

He seemed to think about that. 'Does it have to be *for* anything?' he asked quietly.

'I don't know.' She realised she still had her arm around him and she dropped it quickly, lest he decided it meant more than she'd intended. 'I think we'd better head down again,' she said awkwardly. 'I... well, now I've cooled down from the climb that wind's a bit chilly.'

It wasn't true. Not, at least, strictly true. The wind did have a faint chill in it but she certainly wasn't feeling it now. In fact she seemed to be burning. Her face felt on fire.

They drove the short distance into Avebury and spent an hour or two strolling around the village's incredible standing stones. The last time Mark had taken her there it had been quite late in the day, around twilight, and they'd had the huge circle to themselves with just a few contented woolly sheep for company.

To Kate then, the stones had seemed as magic and secret as they were magnificent, but now, so much earlier, the car-parking areas were crowded and there were tour buses and lots of tourists wandering through the paddocks. The stones still seemed special but the magic was less tangible.

'I'd like to come back later,' she said quietly. 'Is that all right? Once most of the people have gone.'

'Of course.' It was the first time either of them had spoken since his kiss on the hill and she was relieved to hear he sounded quite normal.

In lieu of the lunch they'd missed they ate a late afternoon tea in a lovely café close to some of the stones on the other side of the village from where they'd parked. Kate chose a huge apple and nut muffin which she just about managed to finish while Mark had fresh scones with blackcurrant jam and thick cream.

She took a long sip of her coffee, then put it down. 'I didn't mind, you know,' she said quietly, once he'd finished the last of his scones. 'Before. The kiss. It wasn't that I minded. I was just a bit startled.'

'It's all right, Kate.' He looked serious again. 'We don't have to have a post-mortem. Just forget it.'

'But I don't seem to be able to.' Admittedly it had happened only about two hours before, and by to-morrow she might well have forgotten all about it, but for now she was finding it increasingly difficult to think about anything else. It seemed sensible that they reach some sort of resolution.

'I mean…' she seemed to be having trouble taking her eyes away from his mouth '…well, I think I'm just a bit stunned, really. I never realised that a man could ever kiss a woman without trying to ram his tongue down her throat at the same time.'

Mark seemed to choke. On a scone crumb, she assumed. Grabbing for his coffee, he took a few hasty swallows, then seemed to collect himself. 'You didn't realise *what*?' he rasped.

'That a man could ever kiss—'

'I heard what you said, Kate.' He looked askance. 'I meant, were you serious?'

'Of course,' she insisted, bewildered. 'Mark, trust me. Every time any man's tried to kiss me, that's what he's done.'

'And you don't like it,' he probed. 'The tongue—'

'Rammed down my throat,' she finished strongly. 'Oh, Mark. Blah! I hate it.' She felt her face screwing up at the thought. 'It's disgusting. I can't stand it.'

'Ah.' He looked a little concerned. 'Kate, you're not…you do…well—do you enjoy sex at all?'

'I'm not frigid,' she said slowly. 'I have had an orgasm, Mark. Several, in fact.' Strangely enough, she realised, since she would have found it difficult to reveal that to even her girlfriends, she didn't feel shy about telling Mark that. Her experience with men wasn't particularly extensive—two men could hardy be called extensive, she knew, at least by modern standards—but Simon had been a patient, careful lover and she had found some degree of mild pleasure in his arms. 'But I have to say,' she added gingerly, 'that I really don't understand what all the excitement is about.'

'You don't understand what all the excitement is about,' he echoed softly, his expression suggesting that revelation stunned him.

'I mean, I'm not saying it isn't nice,' she added quickly. 'But it only lasts a few seconds. I don't know why people do such mad things just for the sake of a few seconds.'

'Mad things?' he repeated huskily.

'Well, you know, marrying the wrong people. Having affairs. Getting jealous.' She waved her hand about. 'Men going to prostitutes. People taking risks with their health, exposing themselves to diseases. You know what I mean.'

His distracted nod suggested he did, perhaps, understand a little of what she was trying to say.

'But, Mark, what I was trying to say before was that I think that perhaps I wouldn't mind with you.'

He frowned at her. 'With me?'

'If you wanted to kiss me. Ever.' She felt herself flushing again. 'The way you kissed me before. Well, I don't think I'd mind that. Again. One day. Or any time. To see what it felt like again. If you wanted.'

CHAPTER FIVE

IF HE wanted? Mark just stared at Kate in mute shock, watching the play of expressions across her lovely face while he marshalled his thoughts then debated how best to handle this. 'Katie, I really don't think that's a good idea,' he said finally, heavily.

Her lashes fluttered down. 'Oh.' Her skin had already borne a faint flush but now her colour deepened. 'Well, that's fine. I'm sorry. I didn't mean to be…well, brazen about it.'

Brazen? If he hadn't still felt in shock, he might have laughed at that. There was nothing brazen or obvious about Kate. Instead she demonstrated a delicate, naïve vulnerability that drove him almost to fear for her.

'Let's just get out of here,' he said quietly. Until then the café had been empty around them but two couples carrying trays were making their way towards them now. 'Hmm?' He got to his feet, then held Kate's chair. 'All right?'

'Yes.' But she didn't look at him and the way she walked ahead of him out into the sunshine was stiff and self-conscious, her movements lacking her normal effortless grace.

'What we were talking about last night,' she said abruptly, when they'd walked back through the village to the car park and his car, 'about marriage and children. I mean, you asked about me, but I didn't think to ask about you. I know you told me that you

74

and Janet Holmes have broken up now, but are you seeing anyone else? Seriously, I mean?'

'I took Janet out one night for a couple of drinks at a pub,' he said wearily. Opening her door, he waited for her to get in, noticing, again, that she still refused to meet his eyes. 'No more, no less. I felt sorry for her because old Jimmy Parker had been giving her a hard time and she looked deathly miserable. We've never dated.' This, as he came around to the other side and installed himself in the seat beside hers. 'I'm not seeing anyone at present, no.'

He hadn't been for a long time. He'd grown more demanding of himself, he knew, over the last few years. And more discriminating. He'd never, by any standards, behaved promiscuously, but his expectations of relationships had changed. Where once sex alone had been sufficient motivation itself for him to become involved with a woman whose company he enjoyed, now he found himself more wary. The demands of his body had grown easier to ignore than his need for deeper intimacy and permanency in a relationship. He was, he knew, at some level of consciousness, if not actually determinedly, looking for a wife.

He took the parking sticker off the windscreen and reversed out of the park. 'And, yes, of course I would like to marry and have children. One day. You know that.' He signalled to turn out of the car park and waited for the traffic to clear. 'If I'm lucky enough to meet the right woman and we're lucky enough to be so blessed. Yes.'

'I was talking to Claire yesterday,' Kate told him a little while later as they were approaching the cottage. 'You know, the nurse on—'

'I know who you mean,' he said tightly, wondering where this was leading.

'I got the impression she quite liked you,' she said stiffly.

Mark sighed. He waited until he was parked outside the house to tackle that particular little thorn. 'Don't, Kate.' He opened his door. 'Not you. Don't you dare. In fact don't even think about trying to fix me up—'

'I wasn't,' she protested, finally looking at him then, her lovely eyes wide and hurt. 'I was just telling you—'

'Then don't.' Unable to stop himself, he touched her mouth with one finger, holding it closed. 'I don't want you to tell me anything.'

'She's very pretty,' she said, her lips moving disturbingly against his finger.

'That doesn't mean I'm interested,' he said firmly. 'And I'm not. Claire seems like a very nice woman but there is no spark there for me. I'm not interested. Clear?'

She nodded, meaning he had little choice but to take his finger away. 'What does interest you, then?' she said huskily, when he came around to shut her door after her. 'In a woman? For a man, you're obviously very discriminating.' Mark caught the faint bitterness in that and looked at her sharply, disturbed by it. 'What does turn you on?'

He looked away abruptly. He could have told her exactly what was turning him on, *who*, exactly, and precisely what he wanted at that moment, but since there could never be any future in that direction such a revelation wouldn't help either of them. 'I'm going to change and go running,' he said grimly instead. Normally he would have at least asked if she wanted to come with him—even though she no longer exercised regularly he could have adjusted his pace to match hers—but right now he knew he needed powerful exercise and he needed to get away from her.

He took her hand, turned it over, and pressed the keys to the car into her palm. 'If those journals and books you brought down are so important to you, why not spend a couple of hours reading them? I know we were going to have supper in but it's probably a better idea we go out. I'll make a booking and we'll leave a little after seven. We'll go back to Avebury another evening some time, hmm?'

'Fine.' Her throat made a swallowing movement. 'OK. Thanks. Yes, I think I will get the journals.'

When he got back from his run he went directly to the shower and when he emerged from his room, dressed for going out, a little while later, the sound of water running in the cottage's only bathroom told him Kate must have stepped into the shower soon after he'd finished.

He collected a beer from the fridge and took it outside into the courtyard to wait for her. She wasn't long. But her expression when she came to find him was nervous and he swore at himself for turning her that way.

'Katie, I'm sorry I snapped at you earlier,' he said quietly. 'About Claire. I didn't mean…well, it hasn't been a good day for me. And us, I suppose. Let's just both forget all about everything.' He came towards her, held her narrow shoulders and kissed her forehead briefly. 'Let's go out and have a nice meal and just wipe this afternoon from the slate. OK?'

'OK.' She almost whispered it. 'But first I just want to say that I'm really sorry for putting you in an awkward position—'

'You didn't,' he interrupted. 'You haven't. I'm the one at fault here, Kate. Don't forget that. I crossed the boundary by kissing you. I don't know why I did and I shouldn't have and I'm sorry, but it's done now and I can't take it back. The best we can do is forget it happened.'

'I don't even know why I made such a big deal of it.' She still seemed to think she had something to apologise for. 'I mean, it was just a little kiss. You were probably…carried away by the scenery.'

'Something like that,' he admitted dryly. But he smiled as he spun her around. 'We've got a way to drive. Move.'

Kate had wine with dinner. He wasn't exactly surprised—she did, in his experience, have an occasional one or two glasses of wine with a meal—but he wasn't used to her drinking more than that and although the waiter had been topping her up he got a shock, halfway through the meal, when he realised the bottle was empty. Conscious that he was driving, he'd been careful to have only two glasses himself.

'Another bottle?' the man asked.

He looked at Kate, intending to ask if she'd prefer to order just by the glass since he wouldn't be drinking more himself, but she countered him by ordering a second bottle.

'You don't mind, do you?' she asked when they were alone again.

'No.' He was hardly in a position to object. Even if he worried for her. 'You were telling me about your case last week,' he reminded her. He wasn't happy they were discussing work, given that the purpose of the weekend had started out as being to get her away from Lizzie's, but it seemed the safest subject tonight. 'The child for the renal transplant. You said she had a febrile reaction under G.A. You were worried about a possible allergic reaction to Sux?'

'Oh, in the end we decided she was reacting to the blood transfusion,' she explained, dismissing her earlier concern about the muscle-relaxing drug. 'Her temperature settled when we stopped the transfusion and the lab found some antibodies suggesting it could have been that. She's been fine since. No problems. Her transplant's working well and there're no signs of rejection yet.'

He watched her carefully as they walked out to the car after the meal. She hadn't finished the second bottle but she had made a fair dent on it. Despite that, she didn't seem unsteady, although her eyes had taken on a definite sparkle.

'Don't look at me like that,' she snapped, a while later when they were almost back at the cottage, when he glanced at her to check she was all right. 'I'm not an alcoholic.'

He sighed. 'I didn't say—'

'You don't have to say anything.' Kate was notoriously even-tempered but for once she looked annoyed. 'It's obvious what you're thinking.'

'You're right,' he admitted tightly. 'The thought has crossed my mind. Transiently, only, but it did cross my mind. It would explain why you've been able to put up with that dump of a flat—'

'How dare you do this?' she cried. 'How dare you criticise everything I—?'

'It's not criticism,' he said savagely. 'It's an observation. The place is a death trap. It appals me to think of you living there.'

'Well, stuff you, Mark, because that's my home.' She'd folded her arms defiantly but he could see her hands were shaking. 'And I like it and there's nothing you can do about it so I'll thank you to keep your opinions to yourself.'

Swearing under his breath, Mark turned the car through the farm gate, driving it with less care than he should have over the rough track to the cottage. He felt angry and frustrated and helpless. He didn't know what to say to her. His intentions for the weekend had been clear when he'd started but the whole thing was coming down around his head and there didn't seem to be anything he could do to stop it.

'Kate, just a minute—' He ran after her when she spun out of the car when he stopped it and dashed to the cottage ahead of him. 'Wait,' he called. 'Careful of the rocks. You'll hurt yourself.'

But she was already at the door. 'Can you unlock this, please?' she asked tensely. 'I want to go to bed.'

'Just wait a second.' He deliberately didn't lift his keys. 'Kate, listen to me. I'm sorry I've offended you. I'm sorry if you don't like me criticising the way you work and your home, but I'm being honest. I do hate the thought of you living in that place. I've always hated it but I just…well, until last night I'd forgotten how ghastly it is. You know I don't mean to hurt you but I don't know what else you want me to say. Tell me, and I'll say it. Talk to me. We're friends, aren't we?'

'I don't know.' She tilted her face up to him, her skin pale, her eyes glittering in the pale light filtering from the stars above him. 'I'm not an alcoholic.'

'I know you're not.' He shook his head slowly. 'I know you're not, Kate. Look, however much you drink is nothing to do with me. If you feel like a few wines with your meal, that's fine. It wasn't even that much. I didn't mean what I said about thinking you drank at home.'

'I wouldn't normally drink that much,' she said in a brittle voice, 'but tonight I felt like it. I've never propositioned anybody before. I didn't realise how awful it could feel to be so flatly rejected.'

He knew he should leave it at that, his brain told him to keep well away, but still he couldn't let that go by unquestioned. 'You didn't proposition me,' he pointed out carefully. 'You told me you wouldn't mind if I kissed you again.'

'The same thing.'

'It is not the same thing,' he said heavily. 'Not at all.'

'Asking you to kiss me is almost the same thing,' she countered. 'Almost.'

'I'm not some tame lap-dog,' he said harshly. 'I'm not a puppet, Kate. Certainly not your puppet. I don't offer chaste kisses on demand.'

'I didn't say they had to be chaste.'

'Since the thought of my tongue in your mouth disgusts you they can hardly be anything else,' he countered savagely. Lifting the key now, he unlocked the door and threw it open. 'Now, unless you want to be disgusted, I suggest you go to bed.'

'I didn't say your tongue would disgust me,' she cried. 'I said other men's tongues. I said the way other men kiss me disgusts me.'

'I don't have any special talents, Kate. I'm no different to any other man you've known so don't do me any favours. Go to bed.'

'I don't have to take orders from you,' she shrilled.

'No.' Resisting the urge to kick-slam the door, he instead restrained himself to shutting it firmly. 'You don't. *I'm* going to bed. Goodnight.'

'Don't you walk out on me, Mark Summers.' Instead of going away meekly as he'd—vainly it seemed—hoped she would, she stalked after him towards his bedroom. 'I'm not letting you end this like this. I want answers.'

'In the morning,' he said tightly, 'when you can understand them, you can have them. He put his hand out to stop her following him into his room, bracing his other against the edge of the door. 'Go to bed, Katie.'

'Don't patronise me!'

'I'm not—'

'You think I'm drunk.'

'You have been drinking,' he pointed out, with creditable calm, he thought, given the provocation.

'Not enough to make me forget this afternoon,' she shouted. 'Am I so repulsive, Mark? Am I so repulsive you can't even bring yourself to kiss me again?'

'You are getting this all wrong,' he grated. 'You have everything backwards. For God's sake, Kate—'

'Just tell me the truth, Mark. You owe me that much at least. Is it my hair? My skin? What? Am I hideously ugly and no one's told me?'

Mark muttered a prayer under his breath. 'Katie, go to bed,' he said, more quietly now. 'Go to bed.' He felt as if he'd said it a hundred times but short of physically carrying her there—and there was no way on earth he was going to touch her now—he didn't know what else to do. 'We'll talk tomorrow.'

But she just shook her head at him fiercely, her hair, where it had come loose at some stage in their argument, flying around her face like a silken cloud. 'Answer me first. Am I so hideous you can't bear the thought of sleeping with me?'

He almost laughed. If he hadn't known how much that would have infuriated her in her current state, he might not even have been able to stop himself. As it was, he just sighed. 'You didn't ask me to sleep with you,' he said wearily. 'You just wanted me to kiss you.'

She sagged a little. 'If the kiss was good I might have wanted more,' she protested brokenly. 'I didn't know. I've never liked the thought of anyone kissing me before and suddenly I liked the thought of you doing it. I didn't mean, necessarily, just kiss me and stop. I wanted to see how it felt again.'

'Then ask me again when you're sober,' he said huskily, just about one hundred per cent sure that he was going to regret ever saying that, but still, despite all his earlier grand thoughts about wanting a wife now, not simply sex, unable to stop himself. 'Katie, sweet pea, I can't take any more of this. Please go to bed.'

Kate felt physically fine when she woke next morning. Mentally she felt a wreck, but that was a different thing. She certainly didn't have a hangover but then, since she rarely drank more than one or two glasses of wine of an evening, she imagined her body could probably cope better with the toxic after-effects of alcohol metabolism than could someone whose liver function was already compromised by chronic drinking.

She brushed her teeth and washed her face then squared her shoulders in preparation for facing Mark. After working out that he must still be in bed—she was up almost two hours earlier than she'd been the day before—she briskly scrambled eggs and grilled bacon and took the plate, along with toast and coffee, through to his room.

When there was no answer to her tentative knock, she opened the door quietly and crept over to where he lay on the bed, the white sheet at his hips exposing his broad chest and flat abdomen, one bare arm flung wide, the other folded over his face.

Her mouth dried. Torn, momentarily, between either waking him while the food was hot or leaving it for him to reheat later when he woke, she found that her decision was made for her by him shifting his arm and opening his eyes.

'Kate?'

'Sorry.' Obviously he was good at waking instantly because when he sat up he swung immediately into absolute wakefulness and there was nothing drowsy about the blue glare that zeroed in on her face. Years of on-call work in hospitals tended to do that to doctors, she recognised. She had the same skill herself.

'I didn't mean to wake you,' she explained weakly, averting her eyes from the disturbing breadth of his chest. She'd seen Mark bare-chested before. She'd seen him that way lots of times. They'd swum together often even when they'd been registrars together. So he had a great chest. So what? She didn't understand why she was finding it so distracting. 'I made you breakfast.'

He reached out his arms and took the tray she'd offered him. 'You didn't need to do that,' he said huskily. 'But thanks.' He nodded towards the side of the bed and to her relief adjusted the sheet slightly so it covered him, at least, to his upper abdomen. 'Sit down. How are you feeling?'

'Stupid.' Adjusting the trousers of her pyjamas slightly, she perched on the edge of the bed, folding one leg under her so she faced him. 'I'm sorry.' She'd been flushing all the time she'd been in the room and now she felt her colour deepen. 'I behaved very strangely last night. I'm sorry if I embarrassed you.'

'No problem.' He eyed his bacon. 'This looks good.'

'I shouldn't have put you on the spot the way I did.' He had a strong neck. She could see the slow pulsation of his pulse just above where the curved line of his collar-bone met his throat. She thought about putting her fingers there. She wondered if his pulse would feel warm beneath them. 'No, I shouldn't have put you on the spot,' she repeated. 'That was very unfair.'

'You're forgiven.' He picked up his utensils. 'Are you eating?'

'I've had some juice,' she murmured. 'I wasn't really hungry. Mark, I just want you to know that you don't have to worry about me…saying or doing anything inappropriate like that again.'

'Thank you, Kate.' He smiled briefly between mouthfuls of his breakfast. 'That's reassuring. This is very good.'

'I mean, it's not as if my ego's been permanently damaged or anything,' she said unevenly. His shoulders were very, very broad. She wondered whether, if she put her hands on them, the bones would feel as hard and his skin as smooth as they looked. 'After all, men kiss women all the time,' she added jerkily. 'And we're friends, nothing more. And just because a man kisses you doesn't mean he wants…'

He looked up, held her gaze coolly, calmly, until her eyes dropped involuntarily to his mouth, and then he moved. With a muttered curse, he grabbed the tray in both hands, leaned over to the other side of the bed and thumped it onto the floor. 'Is this what you want?' Shifting forward, he curled his hand around the back of her neck, drew her closer to him and covered her mouth briefly with his own. 'Is this what

you want, Kate? Hmm?' His mouth touched her
again. 'Kissing?'

'I don't know.' His movement had dislodged the
bedding and Kate stiffened with shock as she realised
she was the only one of them wearing pyjamas. 'I
don't know,' she repeated, whispering, but she kissed
him back, her head filling with the warm, male,
freshly woken scent of his skin. She kissed him back
again when he brushed her mouth once more. 'I don't
know what I want any more.'

'Well, you'd better start thinking,' he murmured.
He held her chin with one hand and his mouth
crawled to her cheek, her jaw, the lobe of her ear.
'Because you're running out of time. Are you thinking now?'

'Mmm.' She tipped her head back, closing her eyes
at the blissful sensation of his mouth against her
throat. 'Mark?'

His lips came back to hers. He toyed with her,
catching her tender lower lip between his teeth and
biting softly. 'Kate?'

'This isn't a very good idea, is it?'

'It's a terrible idea.' He lowered her back into the
covers and moved around to come over her so his
warm weight pressed her deep into the mattress. 'A
terrible, terrible idea. This should definitely not be
happening. You taste of toothpaste.'

He was flavoured with bacon and coffee and Mark
and she decided she loved that taste. Stunning herself,
she found herself opening her mouth to him, eagerly,
touching his mouth with her own tongue in eager ex-
ploration, winding her hands in the thick warmth of
his hair to hold him to her.

'I thought I wasn't supposed to do this?' he murmured thickly, pulling away slightly.

'I just want to try,' she whispered, bringing him back to her, winding her legs around his sprawled ones to hold him into her, hungry for him, intoxicated by the thick pressure of his desire against her thighs because that told her their embrace wasn't simply part of him appeasing her. She opened her mouth wider, welcoming the sweet invasion of his tongue, marvelling that a caress she'd always considered repugnant could suddenly be so seductive. 'More.'

Only the more he kissed her, the more he played with her mouth, teased her, touched her mouth, the harder she found it to talk, and eventually, as the kisses went on and on so her mouth felt swollen and tight, she could only gasp out her approval in soft, pleading cries.

Murmuring something unintelligible, Mark slowed his movements, slowed his caresses so the slide of his tongue against her mimicked the deeper, more intimate caress she was beginning to crave. When she tightened her legs around him, her hips lifting unconsciously against him in the same rhythm, he released her hair where he'd been gripping her, holding her still while he let one hand slide between their bodies and into the elastic waist of her pyjamas.

'Kate,' he whispered warningly.

But Kate didn't want to be warned any more. She wanted to be kissed and caressed and stroked. Drugged and heavy from his kisses, her skin burning and shivery, she shifted her legs apart, allowing him the access she craved. Modesty forgotten, she welcomed the startling, sweet invasion of his fingers, taking his tongue deep into her mouth in unison with their slow, sliding movements against her skin.

'Mark—' She twisted her head against the bed

covers, her breath coming faster, harder, as his caresses became more intense. 'Mark—'

But stunningly, with shocking swiftness, the caresses stopped and he jackknifed off the bed. 'Get
dressed.'

'What?' Blinking, bemused, aching, Kate came up
onto her elbows, staring bewildered as he leapt naked
towards the curtains covering the window at the far
side of the window. He'd left them open the night
before but now he wrenched them across the glass.
'Mark—'

'It's Jilly.' He moved fast for his clothes, his eyes,
eyes that had been watching her so hotly only seconds
before, cool now, frighteningly, alarmingly cool. 'I
heard the car. Kate, I'm sorry. It's Jilly.' He repeated
his sister's name again as he fastened his jeans. 'And
the kids. Both kids and it looks like a friend as well.
She's got a key. She'll be here in a few seconds and
the boys will be all over the place.'

'Jilly.' Kate repeated the name numbly, then rolled
over, adjusting her pyjamas as she moved. 'I'll...my
clothes are in the other room.'

'I'll make sure they don't barge in.' He was busy
pulling on his shirt but he caught her wrist briefly as
she spun away, holding her, forcing her to look at
him when what she really wanted was to run away
and hide her face. 'Are you OK?'

'I suppose.' She didn't feel OK. She felt numb and
bewildered and dishevelled beyond belief, but she
guessed he probably knew that and there wasn't time
to explain any more. 'Sort of.'

'Go and dress.' He turned her back towards the
door and pushed her gently out. 'It's all right. Relax.
Take your time. I'll keep them confined until you're
ready.'

Relax? Kate would have laughed at the absurdity of that if she could only have got her breath back. *Relax?*

In the relative privacy of her own bedroom, finding her legs too heavy and weak to support her, she flopped herself down onto the bed and lay back, covering her eyes with her hands, overwhelmed. She was dimly aware of the sounds of Jilly's and Mark's voices, and the excited chatter of the children, but most of all she was preoccupied by the thought of Mark's shattering embrace and how it had felt to have him holding her and exploring her body.

And it had felt good. More than good. It had felt wonderful. She made a soft murmur, one hand lowering to unconsciously trace the path his had taken until a shriek of children's laughter startled her into shocking awareness of what she was doing and she snatched it away.

She was going mad. Determinedly she rolled off the bed, adjusting her clothing and reaching for one of the towels Mark had left stacked on the armchair by the window. She was quite, quite definitely mad. There could be no other explanation for why she was finding herself suddenly transformed overnight from a normal woman into some sort of…nymphomaniac.

CHAPTER SIX

JILLY and Mark were in the courtyard having coffee, the boys nowhere in sight, when she finally emerged.

'Kate!' Jilly, characteristically, leapt up and hugged her tight. 'Mark said you were lying in. Sorry if we woke you. I can't believe it's taken him so long to persuade you to come down again.' She pulled away then, studying her intently. 'Oh, you have been working hard. You're so pale. And you look really tired.'

'I have been a bit,' Kate conceded. 'But you look great.' Mark's sister had always been lively and vivacious and that, along with her curly mop of dark hair, hadn't changed. 'And I was already awake. I just needed a shower before I came out. How's Bob? And the boys?'

'Bob's turned me into a golf widow,' Jilly complained with a grimace, but her sparkling brown eyes suggested she tolerated her husband's hobby. 'And the boys are great. They're here, somewhere—they've just run off onto the farm. We finally seemed to have got Teddy's eczema under control at last.'

'That's good news.' Kate remembered that Mark's youngest nephew had suffered badly with eczema and asthma as well as allergies when he was younger.

They chattered on about the children then Mark, who'd gone inside when they'd been hugging, emerged with fresh coffee and a cup for Kate. She met his probing regard briefly, then darted her eyes away, painfully aware that her face had started flushing. 'Thanks,' she murmured stiffly, taking the cup with exaggerated care since her whole body, including her fingers, felt awkward and clumsy and she was worried about spilling the drink.

Jilly, at least, was still chattering on, apparently not noticing anything amiss between Kate and Mark. 'I simply told his teacher that he was a perfectly normal child and if she refused to accept that then she'd have me to deal with.'

She finished expectantly, looking at Kate as if waiting for her to contribute something and Kate blinked, embarrassed that she'd somehow missed the beginning of the conversation. 'So…what did she say?' she tried hesitantly.

'Well, it's just an ongoing saga, isn't it?' Apparently Kate's instincts had told her the right thing to say because Jilly merely shrugged and took a long mouthful of her coffee. 'I mean, what can I do? After the skin testing they told us it wasn't safe for him to be desensitised so there wasn't any choice. But if she can't handle it, then frankly I don't think she should be teaching children.'

'It sounds like a difficult situation.' Kate, watching Mark, was finding it hard to concentrate again. She guessed it had something to do with Teddy's allergies again and she vowed to pay more attention. She couldn't believe she'd kissed Mark. She couldn't believe she'd lain in his arms and touched him, run her hands across his bare chest. She couldn't believe that she'd let him—well, not just let him but wanted him to—touch her. Wanted him. Wanted him so much that she'd been desperate, longing for him to—

'And frankly I'm at the end of my tether. Are you all right, Kate? Kate?'

Jilly's words impinged faintly on Kate's consciousness and she realised, again, that she'd missed most of what had gone before. 'Oh.' She looked at Mark's sister blankly, struggling to collect herself. 'Oh, yes, I'm fine,' she managed huskily. 'Erm…I'm not quite with it yet, I'm sorry.'

'Blame the boys for the hour,' Jilly said cheerfully. 'We meant to come later but they wouldn't stop pestering me. They wanted to see Uncle Mark.' She grinned at her brother. 'Were you out late last night?'

'Not really.' Kate fluttered her gaze towards Mark when he didn't answer, wishing he would stop watching her from his corner and actually rouse himself sufficiently to contribute to the conversation. 'I suppose it was about…ten, wasn't it, Mark? Perhaps ten-thirty by the time we got back here?'

'About that,' he agreed coolly.

'It's probably that you're still overtired from Lizzie's,' Jilly said, looking at Kate. 'I know Mark's been worried about how much work you've been taking on.'

Kate flicked her gaze at him sideways, disturbed that he'd been discussing her with his family. 'Mark tends to overreact about that sort of thing,' she said unevenly. 'If I followed his suggestions I'd be spending half my life reading novels on a beach somewhere. Don't pay too much attention to him.'

'He never lets us in on any secrets about your love life, mind.' Jilly poured herself another cup of coffee, then leaned forward, a broad grin on her face. 'So, any news on that front, Kate? Are you seeing anybody at present?'

'No.' Kate kept her eyes fastened firmly on Jilly's smiling face, although she was overwhelmingly aware of Mark's silent scrutiny while she considered his sister's question. 'I don't date these days.'

'You're working too hard, that's why.' Jilly

reached out and squeezed her knee. 'But you should make time. You're a beautiful woman, Kate. You're missing out on lots of fun. God knows, if I wasn't married with kids I'd be running wild, that's for sure. Whatever happened to Simon Brent? Last time I saw you I think you'd been seeing him a bit.'

'That didn't work out,' Kate said carefully.

'Oh, shame.' Jilly looked genuinely sad. 'He seemed nice.'

'He was nice,' Kate agreed, concentrating on not looking anywhere near Mark. 'But we really weren't suited.'

'He was quite intense, I thought. Too serious for you, perhaps—'

'Jilly.' Mark's growl was almost a command.

'I was only—'

'That's enough,' Mark ordered quietly.

Kate felt embarrassed about Mark's intervention, but apparently Jilly wasn't offended because she just closed her mouth then beamed at Kate.

'Sorry, Kate. I don't mean to pry, but you know me.' She gulped the last of her coffee. 'Frankly, I'm amazed you're still single. I would have expected someone with your looks to be snapped up years ago while I sat around on the shelf, but look, here I am, two horrible children and a stick of a husband while you're still gallivanting about fancy-free.'

Mark made an impatient sound but Jilly just laughed at him. 'All right. All right. I've said enough. I know. Sorry, Kate.'

Kate wasn't particularly offended, she merely felt a little awkward at the turn of the conversation. Jilly was a born mother who'd be lost without a family to love and look after. They were very different sorts of women. She didn't expect Jilly to understand the choices she'd made about her life.

'Some of us are just destined to be single for ever,' she said lightly with a smile. She stood up. 'I might go and see if I can find the boys.' Dimly, in the distance, she thought she could hear them calling. 'I'm dying to see how much they've grown.'

But before she even made it out of the courtyard a tall boy with fair hair, she guessed the boys' friend, came hurtling across the field next door towards them, shouting.

'It's Teddy,' he screamed. 'You have to come. Hurry. Teddy can't breathe.'

Mark leapt to his feet. Knowing from Jilly's scream that his sister was instantly on the verge of panic, he grabbed her arm, trying to calm her over the hard beating of his own pulse in his ears. 'Where's the adrenaline?'

Jilly kicked her handbag towards him. 'Mark—'

'Go inside and call the ambulance,' he ordered, scooping to collect the bag. 'Kate, there's another adrenaline in the cabinet in the bathroom and there's a full resus kit on the top shelf in my wardrobe.' He directed the boy's friend back the way he'd come. 'Show me where he is.'

Teddy had been stung before at the cottage. That time it had been on his ankle. His reaction had been severe but one shot of adrenaline had been enough to control it. But this time it seemed the bee had got his neck, just above where his T-shirt skirted his collarbone.

He was breathing, just, but he was obviously terrified. His face was red and badly swollen and the harsh, grunting noise with every breath out was ominous. His brother had been instructed what to do and he'd already had Teddy's clothes loosened and was holding his legs in the air to support his blood pressure.

'Good work, Paul.'

'I got the sting out, Uncle Mark.'

'Good boy. Keep holding up those legs. It's all right, Teddy. I'm here. Everything's going to be fine now. Try and relax. I'm going to give you your injection now.' Mark activated the syringe and instilled the small pre-drawn dose of adrenaline into the muscle around his nephew's upper arm, his fingers automatically monitoring Teddy's pulse inside his elbow.

If he'd been confident about Teddy's blood pressure he'd have sat him up to make his breathing better but the pulse was weak enough for him to leave him where he was for now.

'Here's the other one.' Kate came tearing across the meadow a minute later, syringe in hand. She had the resus kit he'd made up so he'd be prepared for exactly this sort of event with Teddy, and she unclipped it and opened it out. 'There's an ambulance coming. How is he?'

'I'll take the green butterfly. Just another small prickle now, Teddy.' He swiftly unwrapped the needle she passed him and, using his left arm as a tourniquet while his right manipulated the plastic sides of the butterfly, he smoothly slid the needle into a vein.

Kate had a small hundred-ml bag of saline run through a giving set by the time he had the top off the tubing attached to the needle and he connected the fluid and gave the bag to the boy's friend to hold up in the air.

Kate opened the flow regulator and let the fluid run into Teddy. 'Good boy, Teddy,' she said softly. She stroked his forehead. 'Won't be long now and you'll be able to breathe properly again. You're doing very well.'

Mark gave Teddy another shot of adrenaline intramuscularly and followed it by a slow intravenous dose of antihistamine. Kate, meantime, between comforting Teddy and reassuring Paul and the boys' friend, was mixing up a dose of hydrocortisone with water. She passed that to him for him to give when she'd finished and he began injecting it slowly. The steroid wouldn't help immediately but the sooner it was given, the better, because it would help prevent any relapse and its effects were long term.

By the time they heard the ambulance's siren, Teddy's stridor had resolved completely, and, with Kate holding the second bag of fluid and taking care his butterfly wasn't dislodged, Mark was able to carry his tearful nephew across to meet the crew.

'I'll go with him,' he told Kate quietly when they were ready to leave. 'Just in case. Jilly says she can't cope with coming in the ambulance and she's in no state to drive.' His sister invariably coped well with looking after Teddy's reactions and administering the adrenaline when she was the only one there to do it, but if he or even Bob was there she tended to go, as now as she stood shaking with shock, completely to pieces. 'Can you bring her and the boys?'

'Of course.'

'Thanks.' He pressed a hard, brief kiss to her mouth, then followed the ambulance officer into the back of the ambulance.

The paediatric registrar on call at the hospital elected to keep Teddy in overnight. Mark knew that if it had been up to him he'd have let his nephew go home since, in spite of the antihistamine Mark had given him, Teddy was fully alert by the time the other doctor had examined him, his stridor hadn't recurred, his blood pressure was up to normal, he had no wheeze, and he'd already had extensive investigations of his allergy in his own local hospital. But obviously this was the registrar's game to call here and the decision wasn't up to him.

Jilly, certainly, seemed relieved that he would be staying in. 'It's different for you,' she protested weakly, clearly guessing what he'd been thinking. 'You and Kate probably see this every day. You can both talk quite happily about cutting open poor Teddy's throat but just the thought of watching you do it gives me nightmares. What if he does need that one day? What if he needs it and you're not there to do it?'

'He doesn't get that bad.' Mark put his arm around her and hugged her into his side. 'I only have the stuff for that at the cottage as an extra precaution. Teddy's never been bad enough for me to even think about doing anything dramatic. The adrenaline did the trick perfectly, as usual. I just gave the other drugs a little earlier than he'd have been given them if he'd had to wait until hospital. He's fine, Jilly. Look at him.' Teddy was happily making friends with the child in the next bed. 'He's back to normal already.'

'I should have been a doctor,' Jilly said thinly. 'Just doing a CPR course doesn't feel enough. I should have gone along with what Dad wanted and been a doctor instead of an accountant. A medical degree's probably the best training you can have for having children. Lucky you, Kate.' Mark saw his sister squeeze Kate's hand. 'And you, Mark. When you and Kate have kids at least you won't worry all the time about them.'

The stiffening of Kate's face was imperceptible, he

suspected, to Jilly, but he was, as always, supremely aware of the nuances of her expressions and she'd definitely been uptight since their arrival at the hospital, and so he took Jilly away before she could ramrod her way through Kate's sensitivities for the umpteenth time that day.

'Sit,' he ordered, guiding Jilly to the armchair beside Teddy's bed. 'I'm going to find a drink machine.' Paul and Teddy's friend had already gone off in search of one. 'Do you want coffee or a soft drink?'

He and Kate stayed until Bob arrived, then he arranged for a cab to come and collect them and take them back to the cottage. Inside the cab, he took one of Kate's small hands in one of his. 'Jilly doesn't mean any harm,' he said heavily, when several miles went by without her saying anything.

'Jilly's great.' She seemed irritated both by his comment and his holding her hand. He felt her making little, almost experimental tugs at his grip as if wanting to escape from him surreptitiously without him really noticing, but since she didn't actually try and wrench her hand away he kept hold of it. 'I've always liked her. I didn't mind her questions. It's you I'm annoyed with.'

He smiled. 'Because I'm holding your hand?'

'You didn't need to kiss me.' She sent him an exasperated look. 'You especially didn't need to kiss me in front of Jilly.'

'Outside the ambulance?' He squeezed her hand. 'That was just a peck.'

'On the mouth,' she gritted, each word hard and precise. 'And it wasn't a peck and you didn't need to do it on the mouth. Didn't you see Jilly's reaction? She just about wet herself. All the way in in the car she was making these suggestive, pointed little comments. She looked so surprised when we got to the hospital, I think she'd even forgotten about poor Teddy. I just know your whole family is going to be talking about that kiss from now on.'

'So?' Mark didn't see the problem.

Her eyes flickered meaningfully towards their driver. 'I'd rather talk about this later.'

Shrugging, Mark let it rest. But he kept hold of her hand all the way back to the cottage.

'OK, spit it out,' he said wearily when she walked ahead of him inside when they finally arrived. 'What's the problem with my family knowing I kissed you?'

'What am I going to say to them next time I meet your mother?'

He shrugged, not understanding what she expected him to say. 'Why should you say anything?'

'She might think we're…lovers.'

'Ah.' He caught a glimpse of where she was coming from. 'Katie,' he chided gently. 'Everyone already thinks that now.' They were in the kitchen now and he leaned back against the bench, observing her shock as he crossed his ankles. 'Or that we have been, at least.'

'Who?' she gasped. 'Who thinks that? Why on earth would you lie to them—?'

'I've never told them anything.' He found her horror bewildering. To him the assumptions made by his family and their friends made perfect sense. 'Kate, be reasonable. Naturally people think that. People, including my family and probably all our friends, think that we were lovers, years ago, that it didn't work out, but we decided to stay friends. That's how they understand our friendship.'

'Well, I think that's ridiculous.' She lifted her arms

up, then turned around, away from him, staring out through the living area and towards the glass doors to the courtyard which he saw they'd left open in their hurry to get to the hospital. 'I can't believe it. People shouldn't make judgements about other people's relationships.'

'Agreed.' But the vehemence of her reaction still puzzled him. 'Katie, it's not such a big deal, is it?' He came up behind her, slid his arms around her waist and nuzzled her neck. 'Surely you don't really mind if my family knows.'

'Kate,' she protested vaguely. 'My name is Kate, not Katie. And there's nothing to know.' But she let herself rest back against him. 'I don't know what's happening to me,' she whispered. 'I don't understand what you're doing to me.'

'I haven't stopped thinking about you.' He swept her hair away from her neck and buried his mouth there, loving the sweet scent of her skin and her shiver at his touch. 'How you taste. How soft you are. How your hair feels when it slides against my skin.'

His heart beating so hard he could barely think, he unbuttoned her blouse and the front fastening of the lace covering her breasts, then slowly, very slowly, let his hands come up to cup her, his breath jamming in his throat as he felt her tightening beneath his caress.

'This morning…you said this was a terrible idea,' she said hoarsely, tilting her head up to him to meet him when his mouth slid sideways across her cheeks to hers. 'You said this shouldn't be happening.'

'Oh, it is terrible,' he muttered, opening her mouth with his to capture her sweetness. 'We both know it is. And this definitely shouldn't be happening.'

But it was too late and she was too responsive.

Knowing what he was doing was wrong didn't stop him kissing her. And it didn't stop him lifting her in his arms and carrying her to his bed. And it didn't stop him touching her and exploring her and making love to her until they were drained and weary and too exhausted to do anything but fall into ragged sleep in each other's arms.

The sex, everything about it, stunned Kate. As Mark drove them into London the following evening, and she had her first, quiet time alone with her thoughts to consider what had happened between them, she tried to work out what it was about it that affected her so.

She wasn't used to always being in control of her life so it wasn't the loss of conscious control she experienced in Mark's arms that was so startling. But she was used to always being aware, to always thinking, brooding, perhaps, too much about what was happening around her, so perhaps it was the loss of awareness, that total oblivion she experienced—the sky could fall in, she was sure, when he caressed her without her noticing—that left her so bewildered.

He wasn't an especially patient lover. He had sometimes spent what seemed like hours just stroking and caressing her but never in the sort of careful, observant, pained way Simon had used to do. With Simon, although she had experienced orgasms, they'd been a self-conscious, stilted sort of orgasm where her only emotion had been relief that he at last had been able to see some result for his patient efforts.

Mark didn't even seem to care particularly if she climaxed. If he became absorbed in stroking her breasts or her thighs or her sex it seemed to her that he was doing it for his own, private pleasure, and not out of needing to provoke some reaction from her. But rather than that leaving her unsatisfied, his absorption in her body and his open, unguarded welcoming of her own, at first tentative but later, that afternoon for instance, bolder explorations had freed her from self-consciousness and restraint, leaving her bewilderingly responsive.

She'd even—Kate bit her lower lip softly as she let herself remember—tonight, when she'd thought they'd been ready to leave, the car packed, most of the lights in the cottage off, he'd silently unbuttoned her blouse, pressed her back against the main door and suckled one of her breasts until she'd climaxed, standing up, just like that, without any caress between her thighs, without either of them even unfastening her jeans.

But then, just as silently, he'd closed her blouse, kissed her with a briskness that had been almost brutally casual, and pushed her out to the car without any attempt at seeking his own pleasure.

Thinking about him now, watching the movements of his hand between the steering wheel and the gear lever as he changed down to overtake a slower-moving car, she could feel the dampness of her body and her legs turning heavy.

'This isn't me,' she murmured, meaning that to be silent, but from the way he glanced quickly at her she realised she'd spoken out loud. 'I don't do this sort of thing,' she added unevenly.

'What, drive?' he asked mildly.

'I don't race off to the country for weekends of wild sex,' she said heavily.

'You think I do?'

'I'm quite sure you do.' She folded her arms, confident, at least, of that. 'It's very obvious you're not exactly…inexperienced.'

'Wild?' Apparently deciding to ignoring her last remark, he sent her a thoughtful look. 'Is that what you think it was?'

'You know what I mean.' Embarrassed now, she stared out her side window at the verge at the edge of the motorway. She was glad, she realised, to be going back to the sanity of work. Only since she didn't think Mark would be particularly appreciative of that sentiment, she kept it to herself.

She felt painfully awkward when they reached the flat. She wasn't sure what the accepted protocol was for this sort of situation. Would he expect sex? She couldn't, in all honesty, considering she'd spent much of the drive back fantasising about him, say she didn't want it herself, but part of her still found the thought of him invading the very private territory of her own bedroom now alarming.

They'd had a brief…heated discussion, as she preferred to think of it, rather than an argument, over lunch that day when he'd told her he wasn't happy about the water-heating unit in her flat, and she wasn't particularly happy about that discussion being revived if he had another chance to look at it. She was quite certain the boiler was completely safe. She'd never noticed any symptoms of carbon monoxide poisoning—the hospital, of course, had to keep a check on such things—the pilot flame burned blue, not yellow, and she'd read somewhere that yellow was a danger sign, and the unit worked perfectly well.

'Thanks, Mark, for the weekend,' she said carefully when he lifted her knapsack and second bag out of the car's boot. 'It's been, well—' She couldn't quite

bring herself to finish that. 'I can manage these all
right. I'm sure you're wanting to get home.'

'Brushing me off, Katie?' The shrewd narrowing
of his blue eyes told her he'd read her doubts without
expending much effort.

'*Kate,*' she corrected. 'And I am tired.' It had to
be true even if it hadn't hit her yet. 'We both have
big days tomorrow.' Because of it being too late now
to walk over to Lizzie's and disturb her pre-op patients for the next morning, she'd have to be in before
seven to be sure of getting around them all before the
start of her general surgery list at eight-thirty. And
since Mark was as diligent as she was about pre-
assessing all his anaesthetic cases personally, it
couldn't be any different for him. 'And you've got a
full-day neurosurgery list tomorrow, haven't you?'

'It's all right.' Perhaps taking pity on her, he simply
bent and kissed her cheek. 'You don't have to justify
yourself. I'll wait here until I see your lights go on.'

She started to say there was no need, that she was
perfectly capable of finding her way up to the flat
without him bothering to wait, but, seeing his expression, she decided it was easier just to let him do
what he wanted.

'Goodnight.' Her face felt bright red as she let him
help her on with her knapsack and she was relieved
it was too dark for him to be able to tell.

CHAPTER SEVEN

KATE'S Tuesday morning list was as usual for Giles and she met the surgeon on one of the general surgical wards early the next morning when she hurried in to check on the baby scheduled to be first on the list.

'Kate, terrific.' His round face beamed up at her from where he was crouched examining the infant. 'I was hoping I'd catch you. I've added two. Both next door. Emergencies in overnight under Prof but he hasn't got space this morning so I said we wouldn't mind looking after them. There's a ten-weeker with an irreducible inguinal hernia next door, came in at six this morning, we'll start with that one instead of this little chappie. Then there's an appendix upstairs who came in after midnight. We'll go straight on to her. She's six. Can't remember her name but she's a real little sweetie and the ward will be able to tell you. Terence would normally do that one,' he added, referring to his registrar who would be doing a parallel list in the neighbouring theatre to him with an anaesthetic registrar and Kate supervising, 'but he's already got a heavy load this morning and she shouldn't be left. Oh, and we're taking Michael Billings back for another look at that his pancreas too. I've put him last. You'd better have a chat with someone in ICU about him too. They had to take out the epidural and they've had problems with his pain relief over the weekend plus he's spiked a couple of temperatures so I'm going to change his feeding line as well. We'll do that before we do the tummy. Frankly,

Kate, he's not looking good this morning. If we don't get on top of this infection in the next twenty-four hours, I'd say we're going to lose the poor lad. Oh, and John was looking for you,' he added, referring to her registrar. 'He wanted your advice about something. He was in here just a few seconds ago—I'm sure he'll bleep you if he doesn't find you soon. OK?'

'Borderline.' Worrying, now, about poor Michael as well as everything else, Kate bent over and quickly listened to her current patient's little heart and lungs, needing to hurry now that she had three extra children to see before eight-thirty. Normally she would have seen every child on the routine list the night before so any additions or complications this morning wouldn't have stressed her at all. 'I'm just never going to take another weekend off as long as I live. What are they giving Michael for pain now?'

'You'll cope,' he said easily. 'Good on Mark for getting you out of here for a couple of days. You've got some colour in your cheeks, at least. He's had some intravenous opiate this morning. Just before I saw him. They're ventilating him again so you won't get much out of him.'

Self-consciously aware that the colour he was referring to in her cheeks felt as if it had probably just deepened to beetroot, she reached for the child's chart and scrawled a prescription for anaesthetic cream for his arm and some midazolam for sedation. 'I'll have a look at him. See you in Theatres.'

Michael, in the intensive care unit, looked flushed and thin and very unwell. Obviously, he'd been critical over the weekend because he was back on the ventilator and he was clearly heavily sedated now.

His father, beside the bed, looked stoic but his mother was crying, and when Kate finished quickly examining Michael with a view to the anaesthetic she'd be administering later in the morning she crouched to comfort his mother.

The other women wept against her shoulder. 'He's been so hot,' she whispered. 'Dr Lamb, we know all you doctors are doing your best but it's just one more thing…' She looked at her husband and caught her breath on a sob as she took hold of his hand. 'And he's on all these antibiotics now but they don't seem to be doing any good. He wasn't breathing properly so they had to put him on the respirator again. Yesterday the doctors took out the drip they were using to give him his food so he isn't getting any nourishment at all now and he has to have another operation today to put one back in again. We thought he wasn't going to need anything more until tomorrow but now the surgeon says he has to operate today.'

'Because of Michael having these temperatures at the weekend, Giles is going to have another look at his tummy and he's going to put in a new drip at the same time so he can start his food again,' Kate explained gently.

Normally at Lizzie's one of the intensive care doctors inserted intravenous central lines in the unit, but when the line was destined to be used for long-term feeding or chemotherapy it was safer to tunnel it extensively beneath the skin before inserting it into a vein. That made it more difficult for infecting bacteria to use the line as a way of tracking into the body, but it also meant that the insertion had to be done by a surgeon in the absolutely sterile conditions of Theatres rather than simply on the unit.

'The doctors here think his infection was probably growing inside the plastic of the line,' she explained.

'Giles is just going to put a fresh tube on Michael's left side instead of the right. It's not a major change to make,' she assured them gently. 'Giles does these all the time. I wouldn't be surprised if he could do one with his eyes closed. And if the bugs were coming from the food tube, then Michael should start getting better pretty quickly.'

'He hasn't even woken up. I know he has to be sedated so he doesn't fight against the machine but he's even worse than he was last time. The nurse told us that that might be because they've given him an injection.'

'Because they were worried about infection, they had to take out all the plastic lines we're using and that included the pain relief tube in his back,' she explained. 'That's why he had an injection this morning for his tummy. When he's in theatre, I'll sort out his pain relief properly. I'll set up a little pump attached to his arm so he has it regularly instead of the way he had it this morning.' She stroked Michael's forehead softly, worried by the angry heat of his skin. 'He'll be drowsy after the anaesthetic, of course, but after that wears off hopefully he'll be a little bit more awake.'

'We're pretty certain it's the feeding line,' one of her colleagues, the anaesthetist supervising ICU, told her. 'His temperature's been up and down but it spiked at thirty-nine last night.' He passed her the latest report from the microbiology lab and Kate noted that, while it showed mixed growth from the line itself, they'd isolated a bacteria in Michael's blood which characteristically colonised in-dwelling lines.

With the inflammation of his pancreas as well as the frequent surgery he was needing, Michael's bowel hadn't been functioning enough to let him eat and so he'd been receiving food via the intravenous line into his neck. With his body struggling to fight the inflammation in his abdomen as well as to heal itself, he needed much higher levels of nutrition than normal, including lots of protein. While it might have been safer, from an infection point of view, to leave the line out completely for another day at least, since Michael was already very frail the nutrition he'd lose could prove critical to his recovery.

'We should be ready to start him around twelve-thirty,' Kate told the other consultant, checking though her scrawled additions to the original theatre list.

'Great.' He nodded. 'Oh, and Kate, John was in here earlier looking for you. He was worried about a child this morning with a possible allergy. Did he catch up with you?'

She nodded. 'I saw him outside.' The registrar had wanted her opinion on one of his children for the morning who was possibly allergic to latex rubber. As a baby, the child had had recurrent bladder infections and had had several investigations of his bladder and kidney system. Because such investigations could sensitise a child to latex, John had questioned his mother about the possibility and discovered that on the child's last birthday a month earlier his mother remembered he'd developed a rash and swelling around his mouth after trying to blow up balloons. A reaction like that was one of the classic symptoms of a latex allergy.

'We're setting up a latex-free theatre,' Kate told the other anaesthetist. Since latex was such a common component of gloves and much of the equipment they used in Theatres, special boxes containing supplies of strictly non-latex materials including gloves and catheters were kept in the storeroom to be used whenever an allergy was suspected. The reactions to latex could be overwhelming—worse, even, than the way Teddy had reacted to his bee sting—so they weren't taking any chances with John's case.

Both her registrar's and her own lists were full and complicated but luckily Giles's short morning tea break coincided with John anaesthetising the little four-year-old with the possible allergy so she was free to move next door and help him with him. Happily the case proceeded uneventfully.

When Giles returned for his first case after his break he seemed particularly cheerful and he surveyed her above his mask with dancing eyes. 'I bumped into Mark outside the anaesthetic office just now,' he announced brightly, holding up his scalpel. 'He's been telling me about your weekend. According to him you've been hiding a very special talent from us. Can I start?'

'Yes.' But her face felt as if it had turned stiff and unnatural and she was glad of the protection of her own mask. 'What talent?'

'Swab,' Giles instructed his senior house officer who was assisting him. 'Cooking. He says your scrambled eggs are out of this world. I didn't know you could cook. You've never cooked anything for us.'

'I get by.' Kate dropped her eyes, busying herself unnecessarily with checking the cuff of the blood-pressure monitor she was using. 'When I have time.'

'Why are you blushing?' Giles sounded amused. 'Suction,' he ordered quietly. 'Kate…? What did you think I meant?'

'I'm not blushing. Get on with your operation.' The

ODA who'd been assisting her was off collecting supplies so, much as she'd have liked to slip away for a few minutes, she couldn't.

'She is blushing, isn't she?' Giles, irritatingly persistent, looked around the operating theatre.

'You are blushing, Kate.' Marie, Giles's scrub nurse for the day, leaned back and peered around the surgeon at her. 'No question about it.'

'Bright red,' the circulating nurse agreed cheerfully.

'You don't think—' Giles, glancing up from the clamps he'd just laid, eyed her speculatively '—you don't think, everybody, you don't think Mark and our own darling little flea brain—'

'Giles!' Kate wailed, but she was too late because, from the startled silence in the theatre and the way every head in the place swivelled to stare at her, no one had missed his point.

'No. No way.' Marie laughed outright. 'Those two? Finally? After all this time? No way! I don't believe it. Besides, Mark's seeing that new ENT girl, isn't he?'

'I say that was just a rumour,' Trish, the circulating nurse, told her confidently. 'Hey, Kate. What do you say?'

'I say you're all mad,' Kate said strongly. 'Giles, concentrate. You're missing a bleeder.'

'No, I'm not.' The surgeon clamped the tiny vessel smoothly, passing the clamp to his SHO to hold while he tied it off. 'I saw it. Kate, my love, you're still blushing. OK, everyone, I'm ready to put money on this. Ten pounds says Kate and Mark.'

'Five says Mark and Kate,' the circulating nurse said quickly.

'Ten on Dr Lamb,' Giles's SHO said quietly.

'Twenty pounds on ENT,' Marie chimed. 'I'll even put a list up on the wall.'

'What about you, Kate?'

They all looked at her and she stared back at them in mute disbelief. 'Fifty,' she said finally. 'Fifty on Janet Holmes in ENT.'

Theatres at Lizzie's was spread over the top L-shaped floor of the hospital. General surgery, ENT, urology, dental, acute orthopaedics and trauma tended to be performed at one end, along the long axis of the L, while neurosurgery and cardiac surgery and the rest of the other specialities including plastics tended to be confined to the specialist theatres at the other end. The two areas were linked by the internal corridor but each functioned independently in terms of having separate staff changing areas, staff rooms and Recoveries.

Because his Tuesday lists were both neuro—a morning list with one of the hospital's neurosurgeons and an afternoon list with another—Mark was stationed at the opposite end of Theatres to Kate, but in the short break between lists he went looking for her.

She needed space, he knew that—he'd understood that the night before from her awkwardness with him when he'd dropped her at the flat. The truth was, they probably both needed space. He hadn't planned anything that had happened between them, and he knew he'd been no more prepared for it than Kate. But still he wanted to see her. He knew her well enough to think that one look would tell him what was happening in her head. And he also knew her well enough to know that there was danger as well in giving her too much time to think.

But her theatre and anaesthetic room were empty

and although the rest of the theatre team were chatting over lunch in the staff room, Kate wasn't with them.

'Ah, Mark.' Giles beamed at him. 'Looking for me?'

'For Kate,' Mark said slowly, puzzled by the sudden, almost expectant silence that had descended over the room when he'd looked in. 'What?' he asked, by way of a general question. *'What?'*

'She's gone to the unit. We just finished little Michael Billings and she's transferring him back. She shouldn't be long. At least, she better not be, the scatty wench, because I want to get on with the list as soon as we've finished these sandwiches.'

'How was Michael?' Mark had heard that the child had had a fever over the weekend.

'His abdomen wasn't bad at all,' Giles told him. 'We had a quick look round, cleaned things up a little, but I'm confident the infection has to have come from the line. No problems getting the new one in. He's critical, still, of course, but if we can get him over this hurdle he should make it.'

'Good to hear.' But Mark, wandering over to make himself coffee while he waited for Kate, was still puzzled by the awareness that, although the rest of them had returned to their lunches, the room was unusually quiet.

Marie Banks, a flame-headed nurse who generally scrubbed for Giles, grinned at him when he sat opposite her next to the surgeon. 'How was your weekend?'

'Fine.'

'Incredible what just a few days away in the country have done for Kate. We've never seen her look so healthy. She's all pink-cheeked and refreshed. She looks like a new woman.'

Mark met her teasing look levelly. 'Amazing how relaxing time away from you lot and a few days' gardening can be.'

'Gardening, was it?' Giles waggled shaggy brows at him. 'And that's your story and you're sticking to it, I suppose.'

'If you've got a better one, I'd love to hear it,' he countered easily. 'Since so far the most dramatic incident of the weekend ended up with Kate and my sister and I spending ninety minutes sitting in a booth in the casualty department in Swindon after my nephew reacted to a bee sting.'

He saw that Giles was considering that, but Marie still grinned at him, apparently unconvinced. 'But despite all that excitement, you would, Mark, remember if at some stage in the weekend you and our Kate just happened to be so overwhelmed with sudden passion you made mad, passionate love to each other.'

'Yes, Marie.' Mark drained his coffee and dropped the paper cup into the bin. 'I expect I would remember that,' he said dryly. He could barely think of anything else. 'You lot really must be bored. The staff at the neuro end are too busy working to sit about dreaming up fairy tales.' He turned back at the door. 'If you see Kate before I do, Giles, would you just mention I need to talk to her about the roster changes for next weekend?'

He knew for sure by Thursday that she was avoiding him. She'd been on call Tuesday night, just as he had been Wednesday, and both days and nights had been busy so that could have—just might have—explained why they hadn't met up even though normally they'd have crossed paths in Theatres at least two or three times a day. But when she didn't turn up for the two-monthly after-work anaesthetic department meeting on Thursday he was certain.

'Apologies from Tim and Kate,' Agnes, leading the meeting, announced once the rest of the staff had gathered in the seminar room adjoining the department. 'Tim's over at Great Ormond Street this afternoon and Kate has *volunteered* to do an emergency case for Prof so he can be with us now.'

Agnes' less-than-subtle stress on 'volunteered' and her pointed, stiff look in his direction at the same time were meant to inform him that there'd been no coercion involved in that, he knew, but it didn't make him any less irritated about it.

The manager ran slowly through the minutes from the last meeting, laboriously disposed of several issues raised since, then—surprising all of them, Mark saw, not least him—the Prof announced he'd decided to bring forward his retirement a year.

'I'll be serving out three months' notice so I'll be leaving around the middle of August,' he told them. 'I thought you all should know before the official announcement's made and I'd like to thank you for your support over the years. Mark, I know you're going to be asked to step in and take over temporarily pending the formal appointment of my successor and you should know you have my support should you choose to apply for the job long term. We might not have always agreed with each other on certain matters but I know you've always had what was best for St Elizabeth's at heart and I and the trust believe you're the best person for the job.'

Surprised, as he was, both by the announcement and the older man's endorsement, Mark thanked him and said a brief few words expressing the staff's thanks for his contribution to anaesthetics at Lizzie's and his and his colleagues' best wishes for his future. Because of the news, with the other doctors wanting to express their own salutes in person, the meeting went on much longer than usual, meaning he had no time to chase up Kate before the end of her emergency case.

No one in Theatres seemed to know where she'd gone. She wasn't in her office and he bleeped her from his but she didn't reply and, given that it was only just after eight and he knew she rarely left Lizzie's before ten, he knew trying the flat would be pointless.

'She was here about twenty minutes ago,' the registrar on call in Intensive Care told him. 'She called in to see Michael Billings. She didn't say where she was heading when she left but she was carrying a stack of journals so you could try the library or her office. Or she might be on the wards looking around her kids for tomorrow. I quite often see her doing that till fairly late.'

Mark decided to give her another hour or so then try the flat. He had his own cases for the next day to see in the meantime and he could fill in time catching up on paperwork in his office. 'How's Michael doing?' From the unit's main desk, Mark could see the child was sitting up watching one of the televisions suspended on a cartoon mouse lever from the unit's ceiling. 'I see you've been able to get him off the ventilator.'

'Near-miracle recovery,' the registrar told him. 'This time three days ago we thought we were going to lose him but he's obviously stronger than he looks. His sepsis has cleared up and according to the surgeons his abdomen's healing well. They're thinking they might be able to close him next week.'

It was a mild night and Mark left his car where it was in the hospital's underground parking area and walked over to Kate's flat just after nine. He'd seen that the lights were on from outside so he didn't give up when at first she didn't answer.

'I wasn't ignoring you,' she complained irritably, when finally she wrenched the door open. 'I was in the bath. Is waiting patiently for two minutes that difficult for you?'

'Yes.' With her lovely face flushed, her fair hair long and damp around her face and only her hands at the edges of the old towelling bathrobe she wore concealing her body from him, patience was the last thing on his mind.

'You've been avoiding me,' he growled, propelling her inside and kicking the door shut behind them.

'I've been busy,' she protested, batting at his hands. 'Very busy. And I got the message you left on my desk about the roster swaps and that's fine.'

'I asked you to bleep me.'

'I haven't had time.' She was still fighting him. 'Stop it.'

'Stop what?' He covered her mouth hungrily, then scooped her up and carried her into the pathetically small cubicle she called a bedroom.

'I have to work,' she snapped, between kisses, struggling feebly. 'I don't have time for this. I've marking to do. I have to do the students' exam papers.'

'I'll help you with them later,' he promised, smoothly dispensing with the robe. 'You've got to move somewhere with a bigger bed.'

'I like single ones.' But her arguments were growing gratifyingly weaker and her kisses more heated, and her hands slid beneath his shirt and across his

back to hold him into her where seconds before
they'd been pushing him away. 'I don't need a big
bed. And there's no room. You're so bossy.'

'I'm not bossy,' he murmured, cupping her en-
chanting breasts and lowering his mouth to the bud-
ding crests of her nipples. 'I'm obsessed. I want you.
And you do need a big bed now.'

'I'm not moving.' She bent over him, whispering
into his ear. 'I'm not moving out of this flat. So you
can call off your mad dog estate agent because, it
doesn't matter how many fancy pictures he faxes me,
I'm not going to change my mind.'

He bit into her softly, just enough to make his
point, holding her tight when she gasped. 'He did say
you weren't particularly receptive.'

'Really? You surprise me. He's not acting like he's
noticed.'

'"Flea in the ear" was his term for your reaction,'
Mark muttered, shedding the rest of his clothes, before grabbing for the tube of body lotion he could see
sitting on the little table at the side of her bed. 'Kate,
I do have your best interests at heart.'

'*Your* best interests, you mean,' she argued faintly,
watching while he read the label then opened the jar.
'That's my new lotion. "Kissing". And it says apply
sparingly.'

'Our interests are the same,' he chided softly, loving the sensitive quiver of her skin as he let a generous blob of the cold lotion squeeze onto one silky
thigh. 'We both want to look after your body.'

After they'd made love Kate made Mark stick to
his promise to help her with her marking. Since he'd
distracted her from it in the first place, it was only
fair, and, besides, he looked so incredibly sexy half-

sleepy with his hair mussed up and his shirt half undone, she just wanted to look at him a little longer.

'What did you think about Prof's news tonight?' she asked while they worked. 'Agnes told me he was going to announce his retirement.'

But instead of any sign of excitement he just lifted one broad shoulder indifferently. 'He should have gone two years ago.'

'But you must be excited about the idea of taking over?' she insisted. 'You know they'll appoint you to take over, Mark.'

'I haven't decided yet that I want the job,' he said evenly. 'I'm happy to take over in the short term and I'll certainly stay deputy, but I probably won't apply to be Head of Department permanently.'

'*What?*' She stared at him, aghast, the paper she was checking forgotten. 'But…why not? Surely making Head of the Department, at your age, would have to be an incredible career move for you?'

'There's some prestige,' he agreed. 'But the trade-off is less time doing the part of my job I love and even more time stuck with administrative work. Right now that doesn't interest me. I'm a doctor, not an accountant. I came to Lizzie's because I want to look after kids, not budgets. Plus, one day I hope to have a wife and children of my own. I want to make sure there's plenty of time in my life for them without compromising my anaesthetic work.'

Kate's head was reeling. She should have known, she knew. She should have known Mark well enough to predict his response. But she'd always just expected that when the offer was made he wouldn't be able to resist. In his position, if she'd had his effortless anaesthetic genius and his talent, she suspected ambition and her career would have won out every time. 'So you're just going to turn it down?' she asked huskily.

He shrugged again. 'Ask me again in a month.'

'But if you turn it down who'll get the job?'

'Depends who applies.' His eyes narrowed on her face. 'Will you?'

'Pointless,' she said absently, her head still spinning. 'I'm far too young.' Admittedly only two years younger than Mark, but then she wasn't anywhere near in the same league, talent-wise. 'Besides that, I really don't think I could squeeze any more responsibilities into my life just now. And, like you, I love the doctoring part of my work too much to give any of that up. In a few years—' she shrugged a little herself now '—I would like to try for it. But not yet.'

Distracted now, she got up from the table and walked over to the flat's little kitchenette area. 'Tea?'

He was watching her. 'Coffee. I still don't like that water unit.'

She pulled a face. 'Two different maintenance engineers cannot be wrong,' she said wearily. One had bleeped her out of the blue to get permission to inspect it on Tuesday and a second one had done the same thing the following day, telling her that *someone* had demanded a second opinion. Kate had a fair idea who that *someone* had been. 'They said there was nothing wrong with it. How did you get that organised so quickly?'

'Friends in high places,' he said evenly. 'Kate, move out of here. Come and stay with me. Tonight. Now. Let me look after you. Come home with me.'

'*What?*' In her shock she almost dropped the kettle. 'Mark, are you…are you asking me to move in with you?'

He stilled, seeming to consider that. 'If I were, would you?'

'*No!* Of course not.' The idea of having him interfering in her life even more than he seemed to be doing already appalled her. She'd simply been stunned he would even offer that. 'Never.'

'Then I'm offering you somewhere to stay until you find somewhere better,' he said calmly.

'Don't.' She lowered her head. 'Don't, please, Mark. Don't ruin everything.'

'Kate...?' He seemed to hesitate. 'What does that mean?'

'It means I don't want to argue with you.' Leaving the kettle only half filled on her little bench, she folded her arms quietly. 'It means that I want you to stop interfering in my life.'

'So caring about you is interfering, now?'

'What else would you call trying to bully me out of my home?'

'I call it caring, Kate. I call it looking after a friend. I call it doing you a favour.'

'Well, I call it being patronising, and pigheaded and domineering,' she reacted, stiffening as the abrupt anger in his tone finally shattered the soft, intimate afterglow of their love-making for her. 'I also call it being belligerent and controlling and insensitive,' she added more strongly when he stared her down. 'And if this is how you carry on with the women you have sex with then I'm starting to understand why none of them have married you yet.'

'I've never asked one to,' he growled, but the hardening of his face suggested her words had stung. 'What the hell do you expect of me, Kate? Think about what happened at the weekend. Think about what's just happened now. Am I supposed to just sit back, do nothing and just let you keep going on the way you've always done?'

'Of course you are,' she raged. 'Having sex with me a few times doesn't give—'

'Having sex.' His interjection was scathing. *'Having sex.* That's what we're doing, is it?'

'It seems a perfectly adequate description to me,' she cried. 'At least the words aren't obscene. Do you have a better way of describing it?'

'Would you care if I did?'

'This is ridiculous,' she argued. 'The technical term hardly matters. The point is, having sex with me a few times gives you no more right to invade my life like this than you had when we were just friends.'

'But then having sex with you apparently doesn't mean anything at all to you, Kate, does it? It doesn't mean I should expect you to return my calls or answer the messages I leave for you. It doesn't mean I should expect you to give up an hour of your busy time to actually meet me for any sort of social exchange.' He strode around room, glaring at her savagely each time he stopped. *'Having sex* with you doesn't mean I should expect you to listen to me when I express some concern for you. It sure as hell doesn't seem to mean I should expect you to *squeeze* me into your frantic working day for any more than the precise time it takes me to actually have sex with you, because you couldn't have moved back to your precious marking…' he swept the papers violently from the table, sending them spiralling to the floor '…any quicker than you got back to it tonight.'

'Those papers are very important,' she shrilled, running to catch them up before they scattered too much out of order. 'I promised Prof I'd have them done—'

'You promised *Prof.*' He looked furious. 'Well, of course that explains everything, Kate. Terrific. It's Prof's marking, but you promised him you'd do it. That lends this whole argument a certain poignant irony, I think. Far be it from me to interfere in the cosy little arrangement you have with the old fool,' he said violently. 'My apologies from distracting you *however temporarily* from work you *shouldn't even be doing.*

'I'm out of here.' He'd left the jacket of his suit discarded earlier on one of the chairs and now he hauled it away and over one shoulder. 'I would say have fun, but, since I doubt you remember what that means, I won't bother.'

'Mark—' Kate was shaking but she didn't want him to go. She wanted to say wait, she wanted to try and explain, to try and make him see how this was from her point of view, and explain to him how important it was that she finished the marking because she had to present at the department's journal club the next day and she had to read the journals she'd been assigned before she could go to bed. But the slam of the door behind him cut off her words and when she made it on her trembling legs to the window a few moments later he was already halfway back along the lane to the hospital, the strides taking him away from her long and unhesitant and furious.

CHAPTER EIGHT

EVERY second Friday lunch-break the medical staff in the department who could get away from their other duties met to discuss recent anaesthetic literature. The consultants and junior staff took it in turns to review particular journal articles, usually those of interest to their particular speciality of paediatric anaesthetics.

Since the Professor had never been enthusiastic about the scheme, Mark, as the department's associate professor, generally chaired the meetings. If Kate could have, today, considering the way they'd parted the night before, she'd have sent her apologies, but since it was her turn to present she knew that would have been unfair to the others.

When she arrived she saw Mark talking with one of the new anaesthetic registrars who'd just started working in Theatres at Lizzie's. She was a very *pretty* new registrar, Kate noted acidly, her stomach clenching as she registered the obvious way the other woman was gazing up at him. She'd only met the younger doctor once before, because until the registrar change-over ten days earlier the woman had been assigned to Lizzie's neonatal intensive care unit rather than Theatres, but this second meeting so far didn't suggest they'd establish any particular rapport in future since the doctor was obviously far more interested in Mark than she was in getting on with the education session.

But clearly Mark wasn't completely bedazzled by

the other doctor yet because he still looked away from her to meet Kate's eyes assessingly as she headed towards the table, and Kate felt the tremble in her legs grow more alarming in response.

Deciding that, in her current state of nerves, fetching herself a hot coffee from the machine at the far side of the room would probably only mean she'd fall over on her way or at least spill the liquid over herself, she simply took a seat at the table as far away as she could get from where Mark normally sat. Keeping her eyes down, although every cell in her body still seemed profoundly aware of him, of where he moved and of the young doctor he was still talking to and when, particularly, he looked at her, she leafed through the journals she'd reviewed with frantic determination.

The registrar Mark had been talking to so closely took the seat beside him and was the first to present a review. A *superficial* review, revealing little independent intelligent thought, Kate noted tightly, knowing Mark in his own decisive way couldn't have failed to register that, although she was profoundly shocked by discovering she felt pleasure at the fact. The registrar was followed by one of the other consultants, who presented a more detailed appraisal on the results of a literature search she'd done on a topic they'd discussed the previous month concerning developments in the treatment of neonatal respiratory distress syndrome.

Kate went as the final speaker of the session. 'I've reviewed all five major journals this month,' she began, careful not to look in Mark's direction since that would fluster her, and aware that her voice sounded huskier than normal but not finding herself able to do much about it. She slid the stack towards the middle of the table for anyone who wanted to have a closer look at them.

'Of particular interest to us is the last in a series of three—no, four, I think—four articles on neonatal anaesthesia, two of which we've looked at previously, in *Anaesthesia* about some work comparing the rate of post-operative complications in inguinal hernia surgery performed under either spinal anaesthesia or general anaesthesia in neonates. This latest article in summary suggests…well, at least the authors suggest, that we should be choosing G.A.—oh, no, of course I mean spinal, we should be opting for spinal anaesthesia for all babies at high risk of respiratory complications. Obviously, that would include all our premature babies.'

She hadn't made notes—she rarely did since her recall of her reading, providing she'd read carefully, was normally very good—but seconds into her presentation she realised she should have because she found herself struggling to remember her outline of the study and its findings.

She took back the journal and found the article, refreshing her memory by quickly scanning the findings as she talked. From the mildly concerned looks she was getting from the other doctors she guessed some of them had noted that her talk lacked her usual fluency, but thankfully nobody commented and the discussion following her talk was characteristically argumentative.

Mark brought the session to an end by reminding them who was scheduled to present at the following meeting. When he finished Kate went to make a quick escape but he called her back and since, with their colleagues looking on, she could hardly ignore him, she was forced to wait, teeth gritted, to one side while he finished his conversation with the young registrar he'd been talking with earlier.

The conversation sounded bland enough—a discussion about a child the registrar had assessed preoperatively the day before—but Kate wasn't blind to the nuances in the assessing way the younger doctor was gazing up at him still, nor was she oblivious to Mark's agreement to go with the registrar to the ward to review the child later in the afternoon.

By the time that agreement was reached, the rest of the staff had left, and once the registrar had made her obviously reluctant departure Kate and Mark were alone. 'I know my presentation wasn't very good,' she said stiffly. 'I'm sorry. I wasn't as well prepared as I should have been but I promise next time will be different.'

'I don't want to hear.' To her dismay, he closed the door, then leaned back on it. 'I don't care about that. You were fine. Even off form you're better than most of them are on form.'

'Still…' she made a fluttering movement with her hands, looking at the floor, at the wall, back at the table where her little pile of publications seemed to glare accusingly at her '…I should have spent more time on the articles. I knew I wasn't feeling as… together as usual. I should have acted on that. I should have at least made notes—'

'Shut up about that, Kate.' The harshness of his order startled her, made her jump back, and when he came to her and took her shoulders in his hands she stared up at him numbly, expecting more accusations, another argument, perhaps some stalking about the room, but he merely sighed.

'Stop it,' he muttered, hugging her stiff body briefly against the warmth of his. She felt him kiss the top of her head. 'Stop fighting me so hard. This situation is as difficult for me as it is for you. I'm as affected by what's happened as you are. Can't you see that?'

She put her palms flat against his chest and pushed herself back, forcing him to release her. 'I don't see why it's difficult for you,' she said tightly. 'It's not as if you haven't had plenty of practice.'

'What?'

'Women,' she snapped. 'Sex. Affairs. Dealing with the after-effects of whatever you've decided you want it called. You're not exactly a novice, Mark. This *situation* might be a pretty unusual one for me, but it's not for you. I've never noticed you finding it difficult to work with your ex-girlfriends before.'

He was frowning. 'You're jealous because I've had relationships with other women?'

'No.' She denied it immediately because the idea was ludicrous. She'd never taken any notice of his sexual…adventures before and she didn't intend starting to now. Just because even thinking about the idea of him then with…that registrar made her suddenly want to throw up didn't mean she was jealous. All it meant was that she was deranged. 'I meant that, given that you're much more experienced than me in such things, I'm sure you're also finding it easier to deal with this.'

'First of all, there haven't been many women.' At her scathing look the hands on her shoulders tightened fractionally. 'Just because, pea, I go out with them or smile at them or talk to them, doesn't mean I sleep with them. Secondly,' he said evenly, 'I have never had sex with a close friend so for me this is as new and disconcerting as it is for you, and thirdly, Kate, no other woman in the world could have prepared me for you.'

'They couldn't?' She stared up at him, bewildered. 'Why?'

'Because there's no other woman in the world so infuriating,' he muttered tersely, drawing her closer, 'or so fiercely defensive and prickly…' he kissed the corner of her mouth '…or so blinkered and so…' he touched her lower lip briefly, teasingly briefly, with his tongue '…blindingly frustrating she just about drives me insane.'

'You're exaggerating,' she whispered, opening her mouth and kissing him back longingly, her breath coming faster as her body began responding to the rough caress of his hands across her back. 'And even if I am all those things, you knew all that before the weekend.'

He stilled. Slowly, very slowly, he drew back from her. 'I didn't plan what happened Sunday, Kate. In fact…the truth is, if I'd had any idea what might happen, I would never have invited you away for the weekend. Right now I'm confused but I *was* happy the way we were.'

'I was too.' She felt herself flushing as she acknowledged that she could hardly accuse him of seducing her. 'And I believe you.' Her voice was husky. 'But I didn't plan this either. I'm still…incredulous that it did happen. Obviously, neither of us was prepared for this.'

'I agree.' He touched his forehead to hers, his arms loosely around her hips now. 'So we need to establish some ground rules.'

'You mean you don't want to…go back to the way it was before?' she asked hesitantly. 'The way you left last night I thought—'

'Do you?'

'No.' She shook her head slowly, her blood seeming to thicken as she saw the answering heat in Mark's regard. 'No,' she whispered. 'I should but I don't. The truth is, I can't even look at you now without wanting to…touch you, wanting to feel you touch me…Mark—'

'Kate, you have to promise me more time,' he ordered, turning her around and pressing her against the door so she held it closed. 'If we're going to do this, we do it properly. For as long as it lasts. I want two nights a week all night and I want you to promise me no extra duties for Prof.'

'You're not to say anything more about the flat,' she said hoarsely. 'You're to stop that estate agent ringing me and you have to promise me you won't ever go out with that registrar you were talking with before,' she finished, her breath coming in soft gasps as he pushed her blouse above her breasts.

'I have no idea who you're talking about,' he muttered thickly, not even bothering to unfasten her bra but simply pushing the lace out of his way.

'Seven minutes,' she said weakly, lifting her wrist above his head to check her watch. 'Ten, at the latest. Mark, there's no time for sex,' she protested, when he plumped her breast in his palm then closed his mouth over the puckered tip.

'We're not having sex.' He swapped breasts, caressing the other one with his hand while his mouth briefly captured the second. 'I'm only kissing your breasts.'

Kate arched against the door, growing breathless with his caresses. 'But I have to be in Theatres in seven minutes.'

'Then unless you want to go there frustrated,

Katie,' he growled, lifting his head only long enough to send her a meaningful look, 'you'd better stop interrupting me.'

Kate spent the rest of the afternoon self-consciously aware that her face felt as if it was red—or at least a very bright pink—but thankfully behind her tightly tied surgical mask her colour couldn't have been as vividly obvious as it felt because none of the theatre staff made any particular comment.

Happily there was also the distraction of the Prof's students. The young doctors-in-training had come along to Giles's extra list that day to watch him close the abdomen on the baby who'd been born with bowel outside her tummy and whose surgery they'd seen the week before.

It seemed they'd all been going along to Neonates each day to watch progress because Giles waved to them when they trooped in. 'You remember on Wednesday we finally fitted everything in,' he said brightly. 'This is all just an anticlimax after that.' He removed the stitches holding the mesh to the edges of the wound, then carefully closed the tissues over it and used a criss-cross pattern of Steri-strips to hold the skin closed over the wound. 'No more pressure than this,' he told them. 'That's all we need. That'll heal beautifully, I promise you. OK, Kate?'

'Fine.' Kate confirmed the baby's oxygen levels and the pressure she was needing to ventilate her, agreeing there was now no compromise to the infant's breathing.

'When will she be able to go home?' one of the students asked.

'Only once we're sure the bowel's working normally,' Giles told him. 'Sometimes in these babies that takes a while to happen, but we have to be sure it's functioning well and hasn't become twisted or matted. Until then we'll keep her on the TPN, the intravenous feeding. But she looks all right from here,' he added heartily, popping a little dressing over the tiny wound. 'What do you think, Kate?'

'She's doing well,' Kate agreed, smiling beneath her mask. The baby might only weigh just over two kilograms, but until Kate had put her to sleep in the anaesthetic room she'd been lively and alert and interested in her surroundings and such intelligence and curiosity in a newborn had to augur well for her future.

But, after finishing that case, the rest of her list was very straightforward and stress-free and she found her attention wandering again. Given all her years of voluntary near-celibacy it wasn't surprising that this… awareness of herself as a sexual being was still taking a lot of getting used to, she acknowledged, her hands busy a few cases later as she drew up a small dose of the drug she would use to induce general anaesthesia for her last patient of the day.

Of course now, however tempting such an idea might have been, there was no longer any possibility of denying her sexuality. Her total, shockingly uninhibited response to Mark as well as the desire she felt for him proved that. But she still wasn't sure she liked that recognition and it wasn't an awareness she was remotely comfortable with.

In a lot of ways, even, despite the exquisiteness of the physical pleasure she experienced in Mark's arms and partly because of her fear that she might not be able to voluntarily give up that pleasure again, she almost, *almost*, wished she'd never discovered that side of herself.

And now she'd promised Mark at least two nights a week. She wanted that much, wanted to be with him at least that much, but she could feel her brain panicking. Her life had been busy enough before she'd discovered sex. How on earth was she going to manage to free up *extra* time to fit it in?

The first week she had to work frantically hard to juggle her commitments enough to mean she could leave Lizzie's at a reasonable time on the Tuesday and Thursday, the two nights that week they both had free, but after that she found herself relaxing a little as she started to find that the mere fact of wanting two nights free seemed to mean that she grew more organised with the rest of her time.

By the end of the second week she was almost into a routine. Mark had—flatly and unflatteringly—refused to spend a night at her flat, meaning in the end she'd accepted his feelings and agreed to go to his home. But surprisingly, when she'd assumed she'd be too unsettled about being away from the familiarity of her own environment to appreciate the change, she was finding it remarkably enjoyable to spend a couple of nights a week in virtual luxury.

Not that his home would normally be classed as luxurious. Frighteningly expensive, she acknowledged with a shudder, yes—the brief contact she'd had with the estate agent Mark had set upon her told her that much at least—but hardly opulent. A bricked, three-bedroomed detached house in a quiet, leafy street close to the opposite side of Regent's Park to where Lizzie's was, the home, despite the price the area would have demanded even six years earlier when Mark had bought it, would probably be classed by most people as more quietly pleasant than luxurious.

Mark, certainly, had plans for extensive renovations once he'd finished his work at the cottage, but still, to her, after the relatively spare attractions of her hospital flat, it was lovely to spend a little time in such a peaceful, spacious environment.

'This is interesting,' she said quietly, after returning from her musings to her reading. It was early Saturday morning and she was fully dressed and doing her best to concentrate although the distraction of Mark's bare chest and shoulders just across the breakfast table from her was making her task difficult.

She'd stayed at his home the night before and she was leafing through one of the medical journals she'd brought with her over the coffee with which they were finishing the breakfast she'd made them. 'This American group's reporting lower mortality in pre-term babies when they use—'

'I've read it,' Mark interrupted, the unconcealed edge to his voice leaving no doubt that he disapproved of her choice of breakfast reading material. 'Only since there's just about as much evidence for the reverse finding, it's too early to suggest any change to standard treatment.'

Kate rolled her eyes at him cheerfully, resigned, after so long and since she rarely actually saw him studying the way she studied, to his gleaming of all current and historical anaesthetic literature by apparent osmosis. 'It's no worse than your newspaper,' she murmured, eyeing the section of Saturday morning paper he held folded in one hand.

'A newspaper I only picked up after you buried your head in that,' he countered, his speaking glare at her journal needing no explanation.

'What would you rather have me do?' she retaliated lightly. 'We've finished eating and I've got to keep up with my reading, Mark. I can't run my eyes over something and have it fixed in my brain for ever the way you can. Believe it or not, but some of us are mere mortals. We actually have to work hard to keep up.'

Automatically, despite keeping her reply good-humoured, she was getting herself into a defensive position for the argument she was expecting but, for once, he let the opportunity to make some acid comment on her working habits go by. 'That new play I was telling you about is still on at the National,' he said calmly instead, referring back to his newspaper. 'The season must have been extended. Shall I see if I can get tickets for tonight?'

She blinked. 'Tonight?' she echoed.

He raised a brow. 'Is that a problem?'

'Well, I was thinking I'd have a chance to get some work done this weekend,' she said lamely. Her research work had been suffering a little, of course—it couldn't not have—but since she was broadly on target again with the objectives she'd set herself for the year she didn't let herself dwell on that. The paper she was writing, containing the conclusions of a study she'd run at Lizzie's comparing two types of day-surgery anaesthetic techniques over the previous twenty-four months, was also taking longer to finish than she'd hoped, but she told herself she'd be able to make up the time by concentrating on finishing it over the weekend since Mark was scheduled to be on call. 'Besides,' she added swiftly, seeking to keep the mood pleasant and counter the cooling of his expression, 'aren't you working today?'

'Only as second on.' He was watching her steadily. 'Chances are, I won't be called out tonight, but if I am I'll just have to leave and catch up with you later. That prospect doesn't bother you, does it?'

'No.' But she hesitated. Being second on call, strictly, at Lizzie's didn't mean consultants having to stay on site because there were still registrars and the first-on consultant available for emergencies. Most nights, in fact, if she was to be perfectly honest, there were no calls at all. But still she'd grown into the habit of staying around the hospital anyway, just in case, using the time when Theatres was quiet to catch up on her paperwork.

It hadn't occurred to her that other consultants might not do the same. 'Do you ever stay on site when you're second on?'

'Only if it's obvious I'm going to be needed,' he said levelly. 'If you can put your work to one side for five minutes, and if I can get tickets, we could have supper afterwards. Otherwise we could have dinner somewhere or perhaps catch a film.'

Kate wrinkled her nose at him. 'You're suggesting a date?'

His expression changed. Suddenly he looked amused. 'Is that so surprising?'

'Well, only because we've never been out on a date, date,' she explained, finding herself bemused. 'We haven't been out anywhere. At least, not since that night we went for dinner at the cottage. Usually I just come here and we…' But she trailed off, then rolled her eyes at his smile, knowing he knew as well as she did what exactly they did, and not wanting to go casting about again trying to find the right words to describe the activity. Instead she wrinkled her nose at him again. 'Well, you know very well we don't usually go out.'

'And?'

'And…well, I really had hoped to get a lot of work done this weekend.' She was tensing herself again for his inevitable reaction to that, but when it didn't come, when he merely waited, watching her, she slowly let out the breath she'd been holding. 'But I suppose I could take a few hours off,' she agreed huskily, checking her watch. 'Particularly if I leave right now and get an early start on my paperwork.'

'If it's that important to you, you can swap tonight for Tuesday,' he suggested quietly, referring to the next night neither of them were on call and therefore the most likely time for them to spend another night together.

'No!' Mark looked mildly surprised and even Kate was startled by how quickly she came back with that. 'No, it's all right,' she added, with more deliberate control, surprising herself with the realisation that she was actually looking forward to tonight already as much as with the understanding that she didn't want to sacrifice another of their evenings for the sake of it. 'I don't mind. Thanks.' She wiped her mouth bare of toast crumbs with her napkin, pushed back her chair and came to her feet, leaned over and quickly kissed his mouth, then smiled at him. 'For breakfast.' She'd already collected her things together and her bag was packed and by the door. 'Don't get up, I'll walk home through the park. It's almost as quick as you driving me and you're not dressed. But I'd better dash. I want to check the unit and it'd be good to get to the library as it opens.'

'Not that you're predictable,' he murmured dryly, but he caught the back of her head as she started to withdraw and drew her back into his arms and kissed her properly. 'I'll pick you up at six.'

'Make it seven.' Kate's heart was pounding but she

forced herself away. They'd made love already that morning in his bed and later when he'd carried her into his shower, but his kiss and the warm scent of his skin were arousing her again. 'I *have* to go,' she said thickly, turning away from him before she gave into the temptation to stay far longer than was wise. 'I *absolutely have* to go.'

By evening Mark had managed to get tickets for the play he'd wanted, a new romantic comedy playing in one of the intimate theatres in the National theatre's complex on the south side of the Thames not far from Waterloo station. Once, Kate recognised, she'd probably have been more bemused than amused by the interplay between the two main characters, but now she discovered that even her few weeks with Mark had given her insight enough into relationships between men and women for her to find the dialogue as witty and enjoyable as the rest of the audience seemed to.

Afterwards they ate delicious Italian food at a restaurant he was obviously familiar with in Soho, and then he startled her by insisting they went dancing at a nearby club.

'But I'm not dressed,' she protested, gesturing down at herself. Because Lizzie's catered for children who might be intimidated by doctors in formal clothes, the dress code was relaxed compared with other hospitals. When she wasn't wearing theatre gear she tended towards jeans or casual skirts and blouses and her wardrobe had never extended to dressy outfits. She wasn't wearing jeans, at least, now, but while the linen trousers and sleeveless tunic she had on had been fine for the theatre and for the warm-evening stroll across the bridge and to the restaurant, the outfit was hardly suitable for nightclubbing.

'It's not the sort of place you need to dress up for,' Mark countered calmly. He slid his arm around her waist and steered her along the street. 'Most people will be in jeans. This way.'

'Prepare to have your toes trampled,' Kate warned when he propelled her from the discreet entrance where they'd been waved through towards a darkened room where a five-piece group was playing smouldering jazz-type music. 'I'm a terrible dancer. I was too young to appreciate the disco era and if it's formal stuff you want I can just manage a waltz because we were taught that at school, but that's all. I used to mean to learn proper dancing years ago but I just never had time. There's no beat to this music. What are you supposed to do to this?'

'Not disco,' Mark murmured dryly, drawing her into his arms and onto the tiny but crowded dance floor once she'd deposited her bag, 'and not waltzing. Just move your feet a little. Like this. Relax into the music.'

Kate blinked a little, doing anything but relaxing as he drew her against his body, feeling startled and self-conscious at first, but eventually growing calmer and more languid as her doubtful inspection of the dancers surrounding them proved that, of all the embraces on the floor, theirs was probably among the least intimate.

'Better?' Mark murmured against her ear what seemed like a long while later.

'Mmm.' She shifted against him languidly, lifting her arms from his shoulders to twine them loosely around his neck, seduced by the music and Mark, her body having grown heavy and warm now. 'I think I could get to like this.'

'More than paperwork?'

'Mmm. Marginally.' She sighed her contentment as he trailed a line of soft, gentle kisses along the uplifted curve of her jaw. 'It's like very long, slow sex standing up.'

Mark made a soft groan and lowered his head so their foreheads met. 'Don't,' he said roughly, 'say things like that to me in public.'

'Then let's go home,' she murmured, smiling at him, 'so I can say them in private.'

They'd only barely been moving but he stilled then and lifted his head slowly, his expression curiously intent. *'Home?'*

Kate, realising what she'd said, felt her smile fade. 'Your place,' she amended huskily. His hands at her hips had loosened and she lowered her own arms quickly, abruptly self-conscious. 'It was a figure of speech. Sorry. I meant your house.'

She almost blundered into the entwined couple next to them as she made her way abruptly off the dance floor, only Mark's hand at her back steering her away meaning she avoided a collision. She collected her handbag briskly, then moved ahead of him out through the club's rather dingy foyer and into the fresh air outside.

'I didn't mean to be presumptuous,' she said apologetically, daring a quick look up into his rather preoccupied expression a few moments later, the brief walk to the corner where Mark had murmured it would be easier to pick up a cab having given her time to collect her thoughts again a little. After all, tonight wasn't one of the nights she'd been scheduled to stay with him. Perhaps he didn't want her to? She'd already stayed her two nights this week. Perhaps he was tired of her? Perhaps the reason for his preoccupation was that he was busy considering how best to tell her that without hurting her feelings? 'I'm happy to go back to the flat on my own if you'd prefer.'

'Don't even think about it,' he growled, stepping forward then to open the door of the cab that had, of course, done a sharp U-turn for them the instant he'd lifted his arm. 'You're a strange little creature at times, Katie.'

'Kate,' she corrected automatically, but she found herself smiling again. His tone had not been unaffectionate and she felt a little thrill at the thought that he wanted her with him perhaps as much as she wanted to be with him.

He was bleeped into Lizzie's early the next morning. The first-on-call anaesthetist was busy with another case and Mark was needed for an emergency operation on a five-year-old who'd sustained a blow to her head at some time during the night. Her skull was fractured and blood leaking from torn veins was putting pressure on her brain, and she needed immediate surgery to relieve the pressure and hopefully save her life.

When Kate got to the hospital just before eight— she was planning to spend the morning in her office working—she called into Theatres to see how the surgery had gone.

'Fairly well, I think.' Siobhan, on duty that morning for Recovery, looked up from the magazine she was reading in the staff room when Kate checked there since Recovery itself was empty. 'But Mark didn't bring her to us. The neurosurgeon seemed relaxed and Mark said everything was fine at his end, but he's still taken her straight from theatre to ICU without waking her up. If you run, Kate, you'll probably still catch him there. They only left about fifteen minutes ago and you know Mark. He won't leave until he knows she's settled in properly.'

'I wasn't actually looking for Mark, I was just worried about the child.' Kate did her best to meet the Irish nurse's amused look steadily. Giles' bland demand, in the middle of that week, that she pay up the fifty pounds she owed him for their hapless bet about her involvement with Mark had proven that it was impossible for anyone to hide anything from the eagle eyes in Theatres. But since then, apart from an occasional knowing grin when he'd seen them together, the surgeon had never made any reference to their relationship. Clearly, though, nothing had escaped him. Nor, judging from Siobhan's expression now, from the remainder of Theatres' staff.

'Well, in case you change your mind about wanting Mark,' the nurse told her cheerfully, eyes twinkling, 'you'll find him here around nine. The on-call registrar's had to go off on a helicopter transfer so Mark's covering an appendectomy we've got booked for then.'

'I expect I'll be busy by nine,' Kate murmured, moving out into the corridor. The helicopter landing area was on the hospital's roof, just above Theatres, and she'd heard the sound of it leaving as she'd been coming up the stairs. 'I've got a lot to do today.'

But for once, alone in her office, she found it hard to settle. She managed to dictate a couple of the case summaries she needed for her study so they'd be ready for one of the secretaries she shared with two other anaesthetic colleagues to type up the next day, but she found herself strangely reluctant to get down to the real nitty-gritty of the work she needed to accomplish.

Restless and irritated with herself for her uncharacteristic lack of discipline, she flicked through more sets of notes, then finally felt her attention grabbed by a note in Mark's neat handwriting attached to the front of one set. The two- year-old child to whom the case notes belonged had originally been part of her day-surgery anaesthetic study but had been readmitted that night with complications from his original hernia surgery and had needed another anaesthetic which Mark had administered because he'd been on call that night. His note reminded her that she would probably need to take account of the extra anaesthetic when collating the results of her study.

Deciding that the best thing for her to do would be to discuss the case now, again, with Mark to remind herself of all the details in case, *just in case*, there was something she'd forgotten, Kate checked her watch, saw it was not yet nine-thirty, collected up the file and hurried along to Theatres to find him.

His appendix case clearly finished, she found him in Recovery. He was busy connecting a fresh bag of dextrose to his patient's Venflon and didn't seem to notice her when she came in and so, after rolling her eyes at Siobhan's brief, knowing grin as she checked the child's blood pressure, she sat on the edge of the main nursing station waiting for him to finish.

After starting the blue pump which would instil the new fluid into the child's arm, Mark moved on to examine his little patient's chest. The child was awake now, looking alert despite his recent anaesthetic, and Kate smiled at his trusting expression as he gazed quietly up at Mark as Mark bent over him, listening to the sides of his chest with his stethoscope.

Mark had that effect on children, she knew. If their positions had been swapped, and it was her who'd been examining the child, she was fairly sure she'd have been busy pulling faces and clucking to try and keep the boy entertained enough to stay quiet and still while she checked his breathing. But Mark seemed to have the gift of inspiring trust effortlessly.

He would be a good father. No, not just good, she corrected herself, Mark would be a great father. With children he was kind, good-humoured, always interested in what they had to say and unfailingly patient. It wasn't surprising they loved him. The woman who was eventually mother to his children—if, that was, she could put up with his bossiness—would be a very lucky woman. A very, very...lucky woman.

'Kate?' She looked up, blinking a little when he said her name, surprised that in her reverie she'd not noticed that he'd finished with his patient and come across to where she sat. 'Were you looking for me?' he asked quietly. 'It's a lovely day outside. As soon as Kyle here goes to the ward I'm free. We could go for a walk in the park, perhaps a picnic.'

'A *picnic*?' Gathering her thoughts as best she could, she frowned at him. The thought of spending the day with him was, unhappily, tempting. But impossible. 'I don't have time for picnics,' she said huskily. 'I've got work to do.' She held up the file she'd brought from her office. 'I only came to see you to ask about this.'

Her tone defensive as she registered his irritation at her words, she pointed out the note he'd attached to the front of the notes. 'I know you mentioned this child to me a few weeks ago but there might be something I've forgotten. Have you got ten minutes to go through them with me again?'

'Make it five,' he said abruptly, his sudden coolness turning her insides cold and making the intimacy they'd shared the night before and the hours they'd

spent sleeping entwined seem like some distant, un-
believable dream. 'Unlike you, Katie,' he said coldly,
'I don't find reading case notes an enjoyable way of
spending a beautiful Sunday morning.'

CHAPTER NINE

'THIS is messy, Mark.' Two weeks later, Giles, looking up briefly from their little patient's traumatised abdomen, grimaced worriedly at the monitor bleeping out the child's heart rate. 'How much time can you give me?'

'Nothing like what you need,' Mark warned, nodding to the registrar assisting him to connect the child's next transfusion of blood to the neck line he'd inserted. A glance at the clock on the wall of the theatre told him they were only a short time into the surgery, but, given that despite already replacing almost half their patient's entire blood volume since his arrival at Lizzie's his blood pressure was continuing to slip, Mark couldn't give any guarantee on how long he could keep the child alive if the bleeding wasn't controlled. 'Possibly none.'

The seven-year-old had come off worst in a collision between the car his mother had been driving and a lorry on the North Circular, the inner orbital road around London. Unconscious, with extensive rib fractures which had caused major abdominal and chest injuries as well as separate orthopaedic and head injuries, he'd clearly not been restrained by a seat belt. The child had come by helicopter to them along with his older sister who'd sustained fractures and facial injuries. According to the emergency rescue crew, the children's mother, who'd escaped with only minor injuries, had been taken to the Royal Free Hospital by ambulance.

'Another four,' Mark instructed his registrar, sending the younger doctor running to call the blood bank who would be on alert awaiting their orders. 'Plus another six of platelets.'

They'd given the boy O negative blood while awaiting the initial cross-match of blood, but the blood loss into the abdomen from multiple injuries including what was obviously a severely lacerated liver—his broken ribs had pierced that along with one lung—was still high and Mark wasn't going to risk running low. Platelets were a special type of blood cell not included in the general blood used in transfusion, but nevertheless required to maintain the blood's ability to clot properly. 'Stat.'

'I need more suction.' Giles, his gloves and gown up to mid-chest level stained with blood, spoke sharply, sending nurses flying for the shelves where the packs were stored. 'Now! Hell. I can't see a bloody thing.'

Mark looked up briefly from where he was checking their patient's lungs around the drainage tubes the cardiothoracic surgeons had now finished inserting. Normally a superbly confident surgeon, regardless of how difficult the job was proving, Giles sounding edgy about his work was not promising. 'Giles…?'

'Sorry, Mark. I still can't stop the bleeding,' Giles said tersely, his hands moving fast as he packed the liver edge waiting for the extra suction bottles the nurses were hurriedly unwrapping. 'This edge won't stop.' He swore. 'The vena cava's gone,' he said violently. 'It might have been just oozing before but it's torn now. Clamps,' he ordered. 'Hurry.'

'Losing blood pressure.' Mark had been watching his monitors continually, but the bleeping alarm on the one demonstrating the pressure in one of the central blood vessels they were using for the infusions warned him that the drop in the child's blood pressure was due to dramatic loss of blood from the liver and the major vein the surgeon had just found rather than heart failure.

'Jim, squeeze those,' he ordered, telling his registrar to force the warmed blood in the two bags in manually by squeezing them rather than simply letting them run through by gravity. 'Linda,' he ordered, when the nurse came running in through the doors from outside, 'get me the rest of that blood and get it connected. Giles, you're going to have to do something fast.'

'Trying,' Giles told him tightly. 'Another clamp,' he ordered. 'Scalpel.'

'Systolic fifty,' Mark warned, hauling over the defibrillation trolley from beside the anaesthetic room door then drawing up adrenaline fast. They had to move fast. The vena cava, draining the blood in the lower body back to the heart, was the body's main vein but it wouldn't be easy to find and control when visibility was so limited. Unless Giles could get access to it to clamp it immediately there was no way he'd be able to replace the blood fast enough to prevent their patient dying on the table. And unless Giles could repair the vein quickly, Mark doubted his patient's heart, already compromised by blood loss and the strain of his chest trauma, would be able to take the extra stress.

'Is he holding?' Giles demanded.

'Barely,' Mark said tightly, sliding another line into the child's neck to connect to the infusion he'd prepared. 'Systolic forty-two. Forty.' Working fast, he kept checking the monitor showing the child's heart rhythm growing increasingly more erratic. 'V fib,' he grated, referring to a rhythm of complete heart chaos. 'Cardiac arrest!'

'Need the sternum split?' Giles demanded, not looking up, asking him if he wanted the child's chest cut open.

'Stay where you are for now,' Mark told him. V fib was at least a more easily treatable rhythm for the boy to go into than a loss of all rhythm would have been, and, unless Giles stemmed the blood flow from the child's abdomen, any heart activity he achieved, regardless of whether he achieved it by open or closed heart massage, wouldn't last.

While Giles and his assistants continued to work frantically on the abdomen, Mark hauled aside the main guards covering the child's chest, shifted out the metal rail supporting them and threw it behind them against a bare wall of the theatre, then slapped a gel pad over his heart and a second one beside his chest tube.

'Clear,' he ordered, and the surgeons released their instruments and stood back for the few seconds it took him to send a shock through the defibrillator paddles.

He shocked the child twice at low voltage, his registrar performing cardiac massage between each shock while the surgeons continued working. 'We've got a rhythm,' he reported finally, gesturing for the other doctor to hold off recommencing cardiac massage after a third shock. 'Giles…?'

'Got him.' Giles sent him a triumphant look as he lifted out the clamp he'd been using to hold the vein along with a long needle holder, the remains of his suture still attached to the needle on the end from where he'd been repairing it. 'The main bleeding's controlled. I'll finish the liver now.'

'Blood pressure sixty-two over forty,' Mark said slowly, his own heart seeming to start beating again as the child's heart rate on the monitor began climbing back again. 'Central pressure coming up.' He adjusted the rate of both the blood and fluid as well as the adrenaline infusions. 'Let's get those platelets in.'

By juggling the child's fluids and infusions Mark managed to keep his circulation stable enough to allow Giles time to finish repairing the remains of his liver and major blood vessels. Once Giles had closed, Mark transferred the child straight to Intensive Care still under general anaesthetic for him to be ventilated at least overnight and probably much longer.

Because of the severity of his head injuries—the emergency CT scan performed immediately on his admission had shown a frontal skull fracture and extensive underlying bruising although no bleeding requiring immediate surgery—it was safer to keep the child ventilated even if it had been possible to wake him up because controlling his blood gases and keeping his blood carbon dioxide levels low that way helped minimise brain swelling from such injuries.

Mark spent time handing him over to the on-call ICU doctors who'd be looking after their patient from then on, then he headed back to Theatres to take over from Kate. It was almost midnight and he was rostered first on call for Theatres until eight the next morning but Kate had been second on and still in the hospital when the pair had been brought in, which was why she'd taken over the care of his patient's sister.

When he looked into her theatre he saw they were almost finished. The surgeons who'd been called in for the child's facial injuries had clearly finished because her face was heavily bandaged apart from the gaps at her nose and mouth to allow access for the anaesthetic. The bulk of the orthopaedic team had finished with her leg fractures and left, and the only surgeon still working was an orthopaedic registrar who was applying a plaster to the child's left arm.

Mark went in through the anaesthetic room and put his head around the door between that and the theatre.

'Kate...? Need a hand?'

'She's fine.' She was turning off the anaesthetic gases. 'No problems. We're almost finished.' She turned around to look at him, her eyes wide above her mask, the chart she was using to record the anaesthetic balanced on her knees. 'How's the little boy?' she asked huskily. 'We heard he arrested.'

'He's in the unit.'

'Will he make it?'

'Abdomen and chest are under control but it's wait and see about the brain injuries,' he admitted quietly. 'Coffee?'

'Give me five minutes.' She nodded to him quickly, busy, now, in her usual efficient, precise way, bringing the child around, and Mark withdrew, leaving her to finish her job.

It was June now, five weeks since the bank holiday weekend they'd spent together at the cottage. He'd been on call for the spring bank holiday weekend at the end of May, and Kate had been on call on the Monday itself so they hadn't been able to get back to Wiltshire, but he hoped they'd manage it soon.

He knew that if he had his way then things between him and Kate would be different. She'd be living in a better flat somewhere, for a start, and certainly working saner hours. But the reality was that nothing had changed. Kate still objected strongly to what he considered his very limited interference in her life.

Despite the concessions she was making in continuing to spend two nights a week with him, there were no signs that she was going to change anything else in her life. And, instead of appreciating the time he took her away from Lizzie's, Kate seemed to have merely timetabled the nights she spent with him into her routine and was simply increasing the time she spent at the hospital on other nights and weekends to compensate.

He'd given up, *for now*, on persuading her to move out of her appalling accommodation and he was on the verge of resigning himself—*unwillingly* resigning himself—finally to not making any impression on her working hours.

To him, the time—the little time—they spent together was special, precious time, time of shared talk and laughter and loving, but it was time blighted by his awareness that, however much Kate seemed to enjoy being with him, she was still keeping tally of every hour he kept her away from work, adding it to some theoretical total she stored in her head, then immediately compensating for it the next day.

Despite his frustration at both that and his inability to make any impression on her life, the sex remained…moving. In spite of the reservations she'd once expressed to him about her sexuality, she was, in practice, passionately, exquisitely and achingly responsive. But sex, however good—however *incredible*, even—wasn't enough for him any longer.

But what did he want from their relationship? Did he want more…intimacy? With Kate? The truth was, he didn't know himself. He freely admitted to being confused. After years of platonic friendship, he still wasn't finding it easy dealing with the unexpected shift in their relationship. And since he still wasn't sure even yet in his own head what exactly he wanted from Kate, was he being unreasonable expecting her to offer him anything?

'She looks pretty good in Recovery.' Kate herself came hurrying into the staff room, interrupting his brooding. She pulled down her mask and smiled at him in a distracted way. Dumping a pile of what looked like student exam papers onto the table where he had his drink, she headed towards the coffee he'd brewed. 'That right leg was badly fractured and she lost some blood but she's young and strong and she'll be fine and I haven't transfused her. So what happened with the little boy? Did he arrest because of the chest injuries?'

'We couldn't keep up with the blood loss,' Mark admitted. 'Part of his liver was pulped and his inferior vena cava ruptured through as Giles went to resect it.' He tipped forward and looked at the top sheet of the papers she'd brought in. 'What are these?'

'The last of the students' exam papers. I promised Prof—' But, clearly interpreting his expression correctly, she broke off and the face she pulled at him suggested any further discussion on the topic would be unhelpful.

She carried her drink to the seat opposite him and smoothly removed the paper hat she'd been using to keep her hair confined, sending the fair strands tumbling around her shoulders in silky disarray as she pushed the stack of papers to one side. 'How bad do you think his head is?'

'Too early to say.' The outcome for his patient would depend mainly on his head injury. He was hopeful the child would be all right, but not confident enough to make any declaration yet. He pushed his coffee away, leaned forward and tucked her soft hair, where it had fallen forward to obscure one side of her face, behind her ear, his hand lingering. 'I like your hair loose.'

She turned her head quickly and kissed the back of his hand, then wrinkled her little nose at him. 'It's too messy. It needs a good six inches cutting off but it's at least six months since I've had time to even think about making an appointment. Mark, what about his heart? Is that OK?'

'He was only briefly in arrest,' he told her, withdrawing his hand slowly. 'His heart's the least of his worries.'

'You still think he wasn't wearing a belt?'

'No question. He went over the top and broke his ribs on the dash.'

Kate shivered. 'If I was a parent, something like that would kill me. The guilt would, like here where the poor mother didn't make sure he was belted in, even if I managed to survive seeing my child critically ill.'

'Accidents happen. You know if it came down to it you'd cope, Kate.'

'I wouldn't.' She shook her head firmly. 'I couldn't. It would be too much.'

'But we see ill children, even dying children, all the time,' he pointed out. 'It's not easy seeing that, but you cope here.'

'Barely,' she said huskily. 'After all these years in the job it still affects me profoundly, and you know it does you too, you know it does, so don't look at me like that. You know you still can't see a child die without experiencing terrible grief. Imagine how exponentially more exquisitely intolerable that must be for a parent. I couldn't bear it. It would destroy me. What if…what if by some…aberration I ended up having children one day? What if something happened to them?'

. 'But you're basing that decision on your experiences here,' he observed, his eyes narrowing at her use of *aberration* to describe the one reason for her ever having children. 'You're looking at a hugely biased selection of kids,' he reminded her stiffly. 'You're only seeing sick or injured children here at Lizzie's. The overwhelming majority of children grow to adulthood with only a few childhood infections to bother them along the way.'

'Mark, theoretically Teddy could have died that day we were at the cottage. You saw the state Jilly was in. Do you really think she would have *coped* if he hadn't recovered? Do you really think *you* would have coped? I don't think so. I think you would have had that grief with you for ever and I think Jilly would have been practically destroyed.'

'Kate, I worry, *Jilly* worries especially, about something happening to Teddy every day of our lives. But that doesn't take away the joy that he brings us. It doesn't take away the joy that he's a happy, loving kid who makes the world a brighter place for him being in it. You try suggesting to Jilly that her life would have been easier without Teddy. You try that and see what she says.'

'What if one day his allergy kills him—?'

'If it kills him then we have all been enriched by knowing him,' he said tightly. 'For that, while we grieve, as we would grieve for ever, we can still give thanks for having been allowed to have him even if it's only been for a short time. Kate, for heaven's sake, you can't keep wrapping yourself in some... frantically busy efficiency shield to protect yourself from life's painful realities. Sooner or later the realities will break through anyway and by the sounds of it the shock could kill you.'

He saw the way she recoiled away from him into her seat, knew his words had hurt her, but he knew, more strongly, that it was time to stop tiptoeing around her feelings. There were things that needed to be said, things he'd wanted to say for years.

'I know you've been through grief in your life,' he said heavily. 'We both have. I know losing your mother the way you did, watching her fading the way she must have faded was hard, but you've let that be your excuse for closing yourself off to the world. You still have to live, Kate. You're still here. You're alive. Stop existing. Stop hiding in your work and live your life.'

For a few, loaded moments she just stared back at him, her eyes very wide and very green and, for once, unreadable, but then he saw she was growing angry and his pulse thickened.

She put her coffee cup away onto the table and stood, the legs of her chair scraping against the room's shiny floor. 'You've always been very good at dishing out advice, Mark.' Her coldness, when he'd hoped for some triggering of an emotional exchange at a deeper level than their usual surface scratching, made him wince. 'But you've lost your objectivity with me,' she said crisply. 'You just can't stand me not letting you organise my life. It drives you crazy, doesn't it? You're so used to women falling over themselves to do what you want, your ego just can't bear it when one doesn't.'

'You're wrong,' he said quietly. He had, a lot recently, honestly questioned his own motivations. He'd asked himself whether his desire to see changes in her life might stem from some selfish need of his own either for her submission or for the smug ego satisfaction he might get from thinking his interventions improved her life. If he had discovered such motivation within himself, he'd have pulled back. At least, he hoped he would have. But he hadn't found that motivation. All he'd discovered was a driving need to see her healthy and hearty and content. 'I want to see you happy.'

She folded her arms, her skin paling. 'Why can't you accept that I'm happy already?' she demanded thinly.

He kicked his own chair back and moved away towards the window, and when he turned back to her a few moments later his face felt as if it had tightened unnaturally.

'Because you've spent three precious years of your life living, if *living* is the word, in an appalling dump like your flat,' he said heavily. 'Because you work at least fifteen hours every day and sometimes much more. Because you never take annual leave because you can't bear the thought of being away from the place. Because you allow incompetents like Agnes Coffee and Prof to bully you into even more extra duties than the ones you volunteer for yourself,' he said forcefully, waving his arm to indicate the pile of marking on the table.

'Because I've seen you practically dizzy from overwork but you still can't recognise that that happens to you. Because you take one public holiday off in a year and even then you bring work with you, and even then you still feel guilty about being away.

'Because you haven't read a book in years, because you've given up even going to the gym when once you loved that so much. But most of all because you're so desperate for human touch and affection that one thoughtless, meaningless kiss on a beautiful day is enough to bring you on your knees to me practically begging me for sex—'

He broke off abruptly, understanding, then, from her stricken expression and his own appalled realisation of what he'd just said, that he'd gone far, far too far. 'Kate, I'm sorry—'

'No.' She drew herself up stiffly, looking as if she might be fighting back tears, then turned away as if she didn't want him to see that. 'That's enough, Mark. You've said enough. I'd like you to leave me alone now, please.'

'Katie.' He didn't know how to reach her. He felt helpless. 'I didn't mean to hurt you. If you just—'

'Leave me!' She wrenched her shoulders away from him when he went to her and tried to touch her, averting her face violently again when he tried to look at her. 'Don't touch me,' she railed. 'Don't you *dare* try to touch me now. I don't want you near me any more. And I'm obviously not as *desperate* for sex as you think I am because I'm calling this…this *ridiculous experiment* off. I don't have time in my life for this, Mark, and I no longer have time in my life for you.'

CHAPTER TEN

KATE thought she did pretty well marking the students' papers she'd agreed to look at after that. It wasn't until the Prof called her aside in Theatres the following day that she realised she might have done anything wrong.

'Kate, you can't give them all As,' he pointed out disapprovingly. 'I mean, the top few might have deserved them, but for the rest of them you've just dished out blanket As regardless. The last time this happened I held my tongue, but this time…honestly, Kate. I know you want them to do well, but this group of students wasn't any better than any other lot I've taught. Could it be you were a little tired when you checked them?'

'Actually, I was very tired,' she rasped. 'And actually these were your students, Prof, not mine. If you remember, on Friday I offered to mark them because you were going to be busy over the weekend sailing and organising your retirement party, so if you don't agree with my assessment I suggest you mark them yourself.' He was still trying to give her the papers but she pushed them back at him. 'Now, if you'll excuse me, I have a very precious child to see.'

Leaving him gaping at her, she pushed open the door into her anaesthetic room and gave Wendy Mitchell and her parents big smiles. The nine-year-old was in theatre for the third time in two weeks for cleaning and a dressing change following surgery she'd had to repair a large, infected sinus she'd developed around her bottom. The dressing change was too painful to do on the ward without an anaesthetic since it involved extensive cleaning of the surrounding tissues, but Giles was hopeful of being able to make this the last clean today before the wound healed up painlessly.

'You'll feel yourself going off to sleep now, sweetie,' Kate told her, smiling her thanks for the syringe the ODA passed her. 'You know the drill, Wendy, love.'

'Ten,' Wendy chanted, her voice slightly muffled by her oxygen mask. 'Nine.' Her long lashes drifted closed over her eyes. 'Eight. Se...'

Swiftly Kate removed her oxygen mask and replaced it with one attached to a mix of oxygen and anaesthetic gases, smiling her farewells as Wendy's parents moved towards the door out into the corridor. Because the operation should be short and uncomplicated, Kate supported Wendy's chin and held her anaesthetic mask manually over her nose and mouth and bagged her rather than intubating her with a tube into her lower airways.

'OK, everyone.' Giles marched into the main part of the theatre, grinning, just as they were wheeling Wendy through from the anaesthetic room. 'Watch out, one and all,' he announced, holding his gloved hands high against his chest. 'Take care. Kate's on the warpath.'

Kate blinked at him as she settled into her seat at the top of the trolley. 'Am I?'

'Violently premenstrual,' he hissed. 'Apparently. According to the Prof. The poor man's licking his wounds in the corridor outside. Had a go at him, did you?'

'I am not premenstrual,' she said stiffly, clicking

her tongue impatiently as she contemplated the sexist absurdity of the Prof's explanation for their encounter. 'Not that that's of any relevance. And I would hardly say I had a go at him. All I said—'

'Say no more. Good on you, flea.' He picked up an iodine-solution-soaked swab and used it to wave aside the beginnings of her explanation. 'Good to see you standing up for yourself. About time.'

'By the way, I won't be doing your new Wednesday list,' Kate told him between cases after she'd wheeled Wendy away to Recovery and spoken to her parents and explained that the operation had gone very well. 'I've spoken to Agnes Coffee this morning and she's sorting someone out for you. I expect Tony Reynolds will be assigned—'

'Tony?' Giles pulled his mask down, looking up from the operation form he'd been filling in, his expression aghast. 'What? The man's a goon.'

'He's a very experienced, hugely competent and skilled anaesthetist,' Kate countered mildly, folding her arms. 'I'm sorry you don't appreciate Tony's sense of humour or his practical jokes but once you get to know him I'm sure that'll change.'

But Giles still looked stunned. 'Kate, this is a joke, isn't it? I asked specifically for you. Agnes promised me she'd arrange things so you—'

'Normally on Wednesdays I have my orthopaedic list,' Kate interjected calmly. 'I enjoy that, Giles. I like it very much. I'm not giving it up and I'm especially not giving it up to take on more of your general surgery. I'm sorry, but that's just the way it's going to be.'

'Kate, I need you,' he protested.

'You need an anaesthetist,' she said gently. 'You're getting one. Tony's very good.'

But Giles, still clearly unimpressed, scowled at her. 'Nasty wench,' he growled. 'Mark's to blame for this sudden spurt of assertiveness, is he?'

Kate drew back sharply. 'Mark has nothing to do with my decision,' she said tightly. 'Nothing to do with this whatsoever. I doubt he even knows about it. Half an hour ago, Giles, you were congratulating me for standing up to Prof. Now you're angry because I'm doing the same with you?'

'At my age,' he decreed, 'I'm allowed to be fickle.'

'At your age, you should know better.' But she smiled. 'I'm still keeping this list. I like working with you, Giles, even if you are a grumpy horror at times. But I'm keeping the rest of my horizons open.'

She was still nowhere, *nowhere* near ready yet to encounter Mark, and since she knew he'd spent the morning in the theatre next to hers she was wary of bumping into him, so she went for lunch in the staff room and dashed away to one of the surgical wards to farewell Michael Billings.

The little boy was scheduled for discharge that afternoon. His pancreatitis had finally settled and despite one set-back to his recovery after his initial improvement with the change of his feeding line—he'd developed another infection, in his bladder this time, and it had spread to involve his kidneys—he was well now.

Initially they'd worried that the amount of pancreas destroyed would render him permanently diabetic, but happily the remnants of his functioning pancreas had eventually taken over producing the insulin he needed to metabolise the carbohydrates in his diet and it appeared he was going to escape that particular complication of pancreatitis.

'We wanted to thank you all, Dr Lamb,' his mother

said effusively, taking her hand when Kate peeked into the side room where they were all waiting expectantly for the final word on discharge. 'You especially, but everyone here at Lizzie's has been so caring. I don't think we would have managed without all the support we've been given. It might sound silly but I think we're going to miss this place.'

'I'm glad you've been happy,' Kate said gently. 'What about you, Mikey? Are you going to miss us or are you looking forward to school?'

'School!' For a normally laid-back eight-year-old, the little boy looked impressively enthusiastic. For the last two weeks since he'd been well enough to participate in lessons he'd been joining the ward's formal teaching sessions, but clearly he was ready for the real thing again. 'My friends sent me letters. I showed them to you, didn't I?'

'Yes, you did,' she agreed with a smile. 'I saw them yesterday.' Michael had been transferred to Lizzie's originally from his local hospital in Essex. His class at school had been sending him regular missives and the latest stack had included drawings of an excursion they'd been on to a wildlife park near their school. 'I thought they were wonderful.'

'The lions were good,' he agreed. 'I have to write a story about the hospital but I don't mind because I'm going to show them all the pictures I've done. Look here.' He scrambled off the bed with creditable agility given that he'd only had his final stitches removed the day before. 'See?'

Kate spent a few minutes admiring the latest drawings he'd done of the ward, then made her farewells and hurried back to Recovery to check on her two patients still there from the morning list.

Siobhan, the recovery nurse supervising her last

case, a little girl who'd had a thyroglossal cyst—a congenital cyst in her throat—removed, eyed her speculatively when Kate bent to examine her patient.

'Did Mark catch you?' she asked. 'He's been in twice in the last ten minutes looking for you.'

Kate tensed. 'Haven't seen him,' she murmured, fitting the ear pieces of her stethoscope into her ears as she put the bell to the child's chest. 'If you see him again, tell him to leave a message in my pigeonhole.' They all had a box in the anaesthetic department, on the Theatres side so there was no need to gown up and leave Theatres to access it. 'I'm busy all afternoon and I won't have time to chase him up.'

'Ah.' Siobhan lifted her brows. 'Like that, is it?'

Kate, lifting away from their patient now she was happy with her breath sounds, sent her a wary look. 'Like what?'

'Lovers' spat,' Siobhan said cheerfully. 'I thought it must be. After all these weeks of being full of cheer suddenly he's looking frustrated. I thought you must have been scrapping.'

Kate sighed. 'Neither Mark nor I,' she said quietly, 'scrap. We do occasionally have our differences, but we're both mature professionals—'

'Kate, you can't fool me.' To Kate's rather startled surprise, the Irish nurse put a friendly arm around her and hugged her quickly. 'I've seen it all, my love. Been there, done that, then been there again, so if you need a shoulder to cry on I'm an old hand.'

Kate had gone stiff. 'Siobhan, that's kind, but really I'm fine—'

'You don't get bags like the ones under your eyes this morning from occasional differences,' the nurse interrupted unceremoniously. 'You've either had no sleep in a week or you've spent most of last night weeping into your pillow. Now your working hours are legendary round here, and I know you were second on call last night, but I also know that that little girl you did last night was the last case all night, so it wasn't work keeping you up.'

Kate understood that the nurse meant well, and she appreciated that Siobhan cared enough to try to comfort her, but the thought that her relationship with Mark had been the object of such close scrutiny turned her stiffly self-conscious. 'This little girl's fine now,' she murmured, shifting her gaze from Siobhan to their patient. 'She's probably ready to transfer back to the ward. I've charted pain relief if she needs it but I doubt she'll need—'

But instead of finishing the sane, sensible, professional sentence begun, Kate found herself inexplicably, startlingly, *mortifyingly* fighting back tears. 'I have to go,' she said thickly, lowering her head as she turned away and swallowing hard to overcome the sudden burning in her throat.

But Siobhan still had hold of her arm and she didn't let her go. She signalled for someone to take over her patient. 'Kate, you can't go out there like that and you can't work in this state. Sit down for a few minutes.' Overcoming Kate's feeble resistance, she steered her out of the main part of Recovery, away from the obvious concern of Siobhan's colleagues, and into the small, private nursing office adjacent.

'Take these,' Siobhan said gently, sliding a box of hospital tissues across the desk to her and pushing some into Kate's hand as she urged her into the armchair behind it. 'Just stay there, Kate, my love. It helps to cry, trust me, I know. No one will come in. I'll get someone to stay a bit longer with my baby and I'll fetch you some tea.'

When the nurse returned a little while later with the tea, Kate's tears had thankfully stopped flowing and she grimaced as she dropped a wad of sodden tissues into the bin beside the desk. 'I'm sorry,' she said shakily, between sniffs, accepting the steaming brew gratefully. 'That was…ridiculous.' She took a fortifying sip of the tea. 'I've made a fool of myself.'

'No. No, you haven't,' Siobhan said softly. 'We all cry round here. Particularly over men. We're all a bit pathetic like that. Was it just a row with Mark or have you actually broken up?'

'I don't even know if we had anything to break,' Kate admitted weakly, feeling her eyes beginning to sting again. 'Last night I found out he never wanted…well, all along he's just been feeling sorry for me.'

'*Sorry* for you?' Siobhan looked puzzled. 'What are you talking about?'

'He didn't want anything about us just being friends to change,' she confided, dabbing at her eyes. 'The only reason it did was because he felt sorry for me because he thought I was a bit lonely and desperate.'

'And were you?'

'I didn't think I was,' Kate admitted. 'But last night he said…some things that made me reassess other things that I've been thinking and after that I was wondering…well, perhaps I was. Perhaps it was only that I just didn't realise it? Perhaps the reason I made work the only thing in my life was because I was compensating for everything else I was missing out on?'

'Firstly, Kate, you're not the lonely and desperate type,' Siobhan said flatly. 'So the man is either deliberately playing with your mind or he's too blind to see you for real. Knowing Mark, I'd say it's the latter, but knowing men...well, who can tell? You've always seemed perfectly fulfilled and happy to me and, trust me, I'm good at picking up on misery. I attract it like a magnet. You have lots of friends. Everyone here likes you a lot. You're bright and cheerful, a bit too easily taken advantage of perhaps, but we all have our weak points. Perhaps it's more that being with Mark has suddenly opened your eyes to other possibilities?'

'But that makes it worse.' Kate blinked up at her, a little bemused at how easy she was finding it to confide her deepest emotions to another person. 'I mean, now that I think I was lonely and desperate, I'll *be* lonely and desperate from now on. It was better that I didn't know, you see.'

'But now you've got Mark—'

'He doesn't want me,' Kate said desperately. 'That's the whole point, Siobhan. He never really wanted me. It was all just some...in his own way he probably just thought he was being kind. He only looked twice at me because he—'

'Felt sorry for you. I remember.' But the other woman made a sort of half-laugh. 'Kate, are you really that nutty? Do you ever even bother looking at yourself in a mirror?'

'My hair's a mess—'

'Your hair's gorgeous,' Siobhan insisted. 'You're beautiful, Kate. Not just on the outside but inside too. The man would be a fool to not want you and Mark has never been a fool.'

'But he told me—'

'You don't take any notice of what men say in an argument,' Siobhan insisted. 'All that testosterone floating around makes them frustrated and they say things just to win, not because they mean them. OK, he's a man, so he's not going to be weeping about it, but he still probably feels bad about whatever he said. And he did look grim this morning. Have you even seen him today?'

Kate recoiled. 'I don't want to,' she said sharply.

Siobhan sighed. 'Despite the fact that at the moment you seem to be thinking of yourself as some sort of pathetically tragic figure, you're not, Kate. You never have been. You're strong and intelligent enough to mean he wouldn't get his own way in everything and that's good for a man like Mark.'

'It's not going to work,' Kate said wanly.

'Not if you don't give it a chance,' Siobhan conceded. 'I know you like your independence, and Mark's the protective sort so you probably find that aggravating, but you'll work that out. Just give the poor man a chance. If you ask me, from the look of him these days he's besotted silly.'

'*Besotted? Poor man?*' Kate eyed the other woman doubtfully. '*Mark?*'

'OK, bad choice of words.' Siobhan grinned and, astonishing herself, Kate found herself echoing that. 'Not the first, but the last ones. Will you at least talk to him?'

'I might,' she said soberly. Not that she knew what she'd say.

'And if after all this you decide you don't want Mark, then I'd like him, please.'

Kate looked up quickly. 'I thought you had a boyfriend already.'

'That's all right,' the nurse said cheerfully. 'He's back in Dublin this week. I'll dump him by phone.'

'But aren't you engaged?'

'It's only a ring, Kate.' Grinning again, Siobhan

flashed her diamond. 'I'd chuck it away in a flash if I thought a man like Mark would give me a second look.'

'I'll let you know,' Kate murmured with a smile, not taking her seriously. 'Thanks, Siobhan. Thanks for putting up with me.'

'Don't mention it.' Siobhan put her arm around her and guided her out of the office. 'By the way, you're ten minutes late for your list so Giles will be having kittens by now.'

'He won't dare complain,' Kate said wryly. 'He thinks I'm premenstrual.'

CHAPTER ELEVEN

MARK met Giles' assessing gaze with bland disinterest over coffee at the end of his afternoon theatre session, but it seemed the older man was not in a mood to be deflected.

'Virulently premenstrual,' Giles declared. 'The wench denies it, of course, but it's the obvious explanation. If a woman's playing up, particularly one like Kate who hardly ever does, I say remember the hormones.'

Mark checked the clock on the wall. Kate had been going out of her way to avoid him all day and he was tired of it. The surgeon had assured him she'd only gone to one of the wards to assess one case with her registrar before coming back for coffee, but she'd already been gone twenty minutes and he was debating whether to chase after her again. The surgeon's warning on her mood, though, intrigued him.

'You're getting old, Giles,' he told the older man good-naturedly. 'As well as rabidly old-fashioned. And if you know what's good for you, you'll keep your mouth shut on any more premenstrual comments or someone will take an entirely justified axe to your neck. Remarks like that are virulently sexist.'

'They're not sexist if they're true,' the surgeon grumbled, helping himself to a chocolate digestive. 'And I am getting old and the advantage of that is that I'm allowed to speak my mind. The girl's been like a gnat with a temper all afternoon, snapping away at me. I can't do a thing right. You know, she sent Prof away bleeding this morning and she's refused to do my new list, and she told Agnes Coffee where she could stick her new roster changes. I tell you, our mouths dropped open when we heard that one. If I hadn't heard her with my own ears I wouldn't have believed it was my little Katie.'

'She's not *your* little anything,' Mark countered coolly.

'Not *yours* either, by the look of it,' the surgeon bounced back dryly. 'I did tell her you were looking for her, but in case you haven't noticed, Dr Summers, the wench is not exactly rushing to your side. Good thing, too. Too many of them fall at your feet for it to be good for you.'

Mark had noticed Kate avoiding him but he ignored Giles's last comment. 'Did she really tell Agnes where to stick it?'

'In three short words or less,' Giles said happily.

'How did Agnes react?'

'Visualise a scalded cat.'

Mark smiled. 'And Prof?'

'Poor man still looked like he was going to faint when I saw him five minutes later,' he was told contentedly. 'She took the wind right out of his sail. He said she threw some exam papers she was supposed to be marking onto the floor and stamped on them though I'm fairly sure he was exaggerating.'

'Stamped?' Mark lifted his brows. He tried, but couldn't quite imagine Kate stamping on exam papers. Scrabbling around at his feet on the floor retrieving them, he could remember all too well, though, and that particular memory made his fists curl.

Still, if she had stamped then he approved. He

doubted this would turn out to be a permanent change in Kate, but, even if she was simply working off her temper from their row the night before, the hint that she might one day be capable of standing up for herself was encouraging. She might decide she enjoyed feeling assertive. 'Interesting.'

'All of Theatres is talking about nothing else,' revealed Giles.

'See you tomorrow.' Mark swung his legs away from the ledge where he'd had them propped and made for the door. After thirty minutes she obviously wasn't going to come back to Theatres. Which meant he had to find her.

He tried bleeping her but she didn't answer and, since she wasn't on call, she wouldn't necessarily be carrying her bleep anyway.

Lizzie's wasn't a small hospital and it took him a while to get round all the surgical wards, Intensive Care and the library. He even tried neonates. Plenty of people had seen Kate—she'd been on the wards earlier checking on her pre-op cases for the next day—but no one knew where she was now. He finished back in Theatres but she still hadn't returned there and the nurses in Recovery had just changed shifts, all of her patients from the afternoon had been taken back to the wards, and none of the new shift knew if she'd been in.

Given that it was barely seven he knew the chances of her being at her flat were virtually non-existent but, frustrated and out of options, he walked across anyway, and simply stared, stunned, when she answered the door after his first experimental knock.

'Thought you'd turn up sooner or later,' she said

shortly, standing back to let him in. 'Come to survey the damage?'

'I can't see any.' He surveyed her carefully, taking in the damp tendrils of hair around her flushed face, the sports gear and the towel round her neck. *'Aerobics?'*

'Yes.'

'And?'

'My first class just about killed me,' she said coolly, leaving him to stroll through into her bedroom. 'But I'll get there in time. There was a big queue at the gym showers so I've come home for one.' Obviously reading his intent as he made to follow her, she turned around at the door. 'Don't even think about it,' she ordered, closing her door.

His brows raised, but he waited, where she wanted, helping himself from her fridge to one of the beers she'd bought for him several weeks before, then turning on the television in a vain attempt to distract himself from images provoked by the sound of water running through the water heater.

Eventually the water shut off and when she emerged a while later, wearing faded jeans and a T-shirt that cupped her obviously bare breasts in a way that was probably raising his blood pressure more than a few degrees, she registered the way he stood for her, waiting, with a cool look, but simply walked to her fridge and retrieved a bottle of water.

She drank half of it, direct from the bottle, then leaned back against the table and folded her arms, eyeing him assessingly, the water bottle still in hand. 'Did you agree to have sex with me that first time because you felt sorry for me?'

'That was part of it.' Mark met her regard calmly. 'Although I was more worried than sorry.'

She lifted one brow. 'Worried?'

'You'd seemed…brittle. I was worried about you. You seemed to be becoming even more obsessed with your work than usual. Sex, at least, wasn't work. Or at least that's how I rationalised it to myself.'

'You needed to do that, then? To rationalise it?'

'Of course.'

'So there was no…desire on your part?'

'Of course there was desire.' As always, her absolute ignorance of her own attractiveness and of a man's susceptibility to that bemused him. 'There's always been desire, Kate. What I'm explaining is why I allowed that to overcome my better judgement about what happened.'

She finished the water, then dropped the empty bottle into the sink. 'I didn't sleep after our…talk last night.'

'You think I did?' he said heavily. He'd spent half the night pacing his office at Lizzie's and the other part doing the same at home.

'I think you got a lot of things right.'

'I went too far.'

'I don't think so.' She tilted her chin up to him. It was still daylight outside but with the window behind her her face was too shadowed for him to read her expression properly. But he could see how stiffly she was holding herself. 'I think perhaps I needed that. I think perhaps I needed to be shocked into looking at myself through your eyes. I was…upset by what I saw. I think you exaggerated reality somewhat, but still it wasn't a very pretty picture. I've decided to make some changes in my life. I'm going to move out of here, for a start. I'm going to find somewhere nicer, a little further away from Lizzie's, and from now on I'm going to be more assertive at work. It's strange, isn't it, that I can be assertive in my private life yet have such problems being the same in my professional? But I'm going to try and change that now. I'm going to be careful that I don't allow myself to be taken advantage off. I've started doing that, a little, already, and I like the feeling. I'm confident now that I can be that way yet still be a very good doctor for my patients.'

'Good. I'm glad.' Such a declaration was exactly what he'd dreamed of hearing but her calm coolness kept him tense. Although the stiff formality of their exchange, considering their normal ease, seemed strained and unnatural, her tightness warned him that that was how she wanted it kept. 'So what about us?'

'I'm not doing this for you, Mark.' Her tone went so far as to suggest he was irrelevant. 'This is all for me.'

He shook his head briefly, dismissing that because of course it was for her. His concern, his worry, had always been for her. 'And us, Kate?' he repeated, needing to know her answer to that.

'Mark, are you, by any chance, in love with me?'

He hadn't been expecting that, hadn't even allowed himself to consider that, not ever, because the consequences of discovering he might be would always have been so disastrous, and the shock of the question made him suck in his breath.

It wasn't a response—it wasn't any sort of response, not even the start of one, but clearly Kate saw it as one because her lashes came down and she lowered her head quickly.

'You needn't worry, I didn't expect you to say yes,' she said quietly, her voice sounding a little muffled now. 'I only asked because someone today said... well, not even that really, she said besotted more than...well, that doesn't matter now, I just thought I should rule that out right at the beginning now. Before we went on to anything else. Do you still want to see me? Like we have been, I mean?'

'Yes.' Still reeling from her other question, this one, at least, he didn't even need to think about. 'Are you the same?'

'It's a little bit more complicated for me.'

'Complicated?' He frowned. 'Why? What do you mean?'

'It means I really need to think about that.' She turned away from him and braced her arms against the edges of her kitchenette's cooker. 'I think it might be best for me if for the time being we don't have sex, if you don't mind.'

'You don't have to appease me, Kate.' Her evasiveness irritated him suddenly because he thought he understood the reason for it. He didn't want to lose her but it made no sense to him that she should finally become assertive at work if, at the same time, the price was timidity in her private life. 'If you tell me it's off, it's off. I won't be happy, but I'm not about to shatter into pieces on the floor.'

'I never imagined you would,' she gritted, sounding irritated now, but he didn't mind because at least that was a genuine, honest emotion after the last half-hour of courtesy so nervous and controlled it scraped his nerves. 'Since I'm sure it won't take you five minutes to find a pair of suitably welcoming arms to comfort you.'

'You're jealous now?' He shook his head, coming slowly towards her, newly bemused again. 'You're jealous of the mythical possibility I might want to see another woman? Katie…?' He took her shoulders, held her just there, his touch carefully platonic. 'Hmm? You're confusing me, pea. Talk to me. What's going on?'

'I think I've fallen in love with you.'

He dropped his arms. 'What?'

'I think I love you,' she repeated harshly, turning slowly around to face him, her face deathly pale, her eyes glowing huge and green. 'I think that over the last few weeks I might have…well, fallen in love with you.'

'You *think*?'

'I have.' She almost shouted at him.

'That's the complication?' he demanded.

'It's a pretty good one,' she snapped.

He felt numb. 'What…when? When exactly?'

'What does it matter when?' She looked annoyed. 'Timing doesn't make any difference, Mark. What a stupid question.'

'Then here's another one for you.' He spun away from her and strode back to the window at the far side of the little room. 'What the hell happens now?'

'Why should anything happen?' When he turned around her eyes were spitting fire and she had her hands on her hips. 'I don't see what difference it makes. I won't be mooning around pathetically after you at work if that's what you're worried about.'

'It isn't,' he growled. 'Kate, you have to give me time to think about this. It never occurred to me you could ever—' He broke off, rubbed his hands across his eyes. 'I have to think. I want children. If it turns out I can't have them for physical reasons, then I can live with that, but I don't know if I can just never try. I don't want them just to happen because of some *aberration*—'

'I'm not asking you to marry me, Mark.' She looked incredulous that he'd even contemplated that. 'I don't even want to get married. And if I did, I certainly wouldn't choose a man who didn't love me.'

He frowned. 'I didn't say—'

'You didn't have to say,' she snapped. 'I read your face.'

'Don't get snappy with me,' he countered. 'This isn't my fault, Katie. I didn't ask for this.'

'Oh, and you think *I* did?' She looked enraged. 'This,' she hissed, 'is the last thing in the world I wanted. And I will get *snappy* any time I choose to get snappy, Mark Summers, and I *choose* to be snappy now.'

She stamped—and at that moment he could quite believe she'd probably stamped on the Prof's exam papers that morning—to the door of the flat and wrenched it open. 'And I've had just about enough of you for now, thank you very much, so you can just get out.'

Deliberately slowing his breathing to calm himself, for despite his shock he couldn't not have been powerfully aroused by the gentle bounce of her breasts beneath her T-shirt then, Mark walked silently towards her.

He could tell from her triumph that she thought she'd won, only when he slammed the door shut, keeping them both inside, her expression grew fractionally alarmed. 'I'm not,' he gritted, 'leaving. You can't end every argument, Katie, by throwing me out.'

'It's not Katie, it's Kate,' she gritted. 'You have no idea how annoying I find Katie.'

'I know pretty well,' he remarked evenly. 'You know you're incredibly sexy when you're angry.'

Her face flushed red. 'If you think—'

'If I think what, Katie? Hmm?' He backed her against the door he'd just slammed, taking her hands and holding them above her head in one of his while he lowered his mouth to her throat. 'You're wearing "Kissing". You know that turns me on.'

'I only put it on because of my shower,' she protested faintly, twisting her head slowly although she made no other move to evade him. 'Not for you. It's just to soften my skin.'

'I love your skin.' He ran his free hand down her throat appreciatively, then slid his palm inside the neck of her T-shirt to cup her bare breast, his pulse thumping as her breath began to come more quickly. 'I love your breasts.' He caressed one slowly, closing his mouth over her partly open one hungrily. 'I love holding them,' he murmured, shifting his mouth to her jaw. 'I love stroking them and touching them. I love how this makes you shiver like this.'

'It isn't fair,' she whispered, between kisses. 'It isn't fair that you can do this to me. I didn't want this.'

'Liar.' Mark released her hands to leave his own free to unfasten her jeans and haul them off along with her panties. Too aroused then by the soft pleas she made against him at the slow slide of his fingers to wait any longer for what he craved, he swiftly shed his own clothes and lifted her, fitting himself tightly into her softness and protecting her head with his hand as he thrust her back against the door.

When the sun on her face woke her very early the next morning Kate opened her eyes and looked straight into Mark's. He was lying on his side, his legs entwined with hers, completely awake, watching her.

She smiled at him. 'You stayed,' she said wondrously, reaching out to touch his cheek with her hand. It was the first time he'd spent a night at her flat. 'I thought you hated my bed.'

He turned his head, pressing his warm mouth to her palm. 'I want to marry you.'

'No, you don't.' She pulled her hand back sharply, her mood changing abruptly. 'You know you don't. Don't be *kind*, Mark. I can't bear you to be kind to me. It's almost as bad as you feeling sorry for me and it just makes everything worse.'

'I'm not being kind.' He trailed his fingers idly down the middle of her chest to her tummy. 'I'm being irrational.'

'Well, don't.' Pushing his hand away, she scrambled up and over him and off the bed, grabbing the towel she'd left drying the night before over a chair to cover her. 'I already told you I didn't want to get married.'

'You'll change your mind.' With his usual lack of self-consciousness about his own nudity, he shoved back the covers, swung out of the bed, and came after her. 'Eventually. I'm not giving you up, Katie.'

Kate, backing, muttered something very rude. '*Kate,*' she said strongly, when he lifted his brows in mock surprise. 'And I didn't say you had to give me up, at least not until you want to. All I said was that I wouldn't marry you.'

'That wasn't *all*,' he reminded her softly. 'You said you loved me.'

'And you said you didn't love me back.'

'No, I didn't.'

'Yes, you did.' Still backing as he continued to advance, she frowned, trying to remember what it was, exactly, that he had said. 'I'm sure you did.'

'I said I needed to think,' he said calmly. 'I've had eight hours. The way you can be about work drives me crazy, but it hasn't stopped me loving you. I'm going to stay on as deputy and keep up my teaching work but I'm turning down Head of Department. That'll mean I have time at home with you when you're there without sacrificing anaesthetic time and I'm going to marry you. I love you, Katie—'

'Kate,' she said vaguely, her head spinning.

'I'm going to marry you, *Katie*.' He smiled. 'I'm going to marry you and love you and take care of you the way someone has to take care of you.'

She drew a quick breath. 'I'm perfectly capable of taking care of myself—'

'No,' he said quietly, 'you're not.' His eyes gleamed blue triumph when she came up hard against the far wall of her living room. 'We both know you're not. At least not the way you should take care of yourself. You're starting to get there, perhaps, but that could slip away. You need me to make sure you stay sane and I need you because I just need you.'

'I need you to go away,' she protested weakly, putting up her hands to ward him off, but of course he barely even noticed them and he put his hands either side of her head and lowered his mouth to the curve of her throat. 'I need you to be rational again.'

'I don't want to be rational.' His warm mouth tracked up to her jaw. 'I don't care if you drive me to madness. I want to make love to you until you're old and little and wrinkled and then I want to keep on making love to you.'

'Mark, that's not all you want,' she said weakly.

'No.' The corners of his mouth tightened and she knew that he understood what she'd meant. 'I also want to make you pregnant with my children but I want you more. I've been thinking about that too. I can live without having children of my own, Katie.' He bit her ear, kissed her when she shivered. 'I've got Teddy and Paul and our patients and I can make do. But I don't want to live without you. I love you. Marry me.'

Kate twisted her head away, dampening her lips with a nervous tongue. 'There's just one little thing I should say…about children. Lately I seem to be, well…' she didn't know how to explain exactly '…I'm noticing pregnant women everywhere. I've been finding myself staring at their tummies. I've been wondering if perhaps I wasn't becoming a little bit clucky. I mean, I know I'm going to be cutting down on the amount of time I spend in my off-duty hours at Lizzie's, but still heaven knows how I could possibly fit children into my life at the moment, even one, let alone two or three. I'm busy enough already with work and with you and with all this sex, and now of course I'm determined to start going back to the gym, but—'

'I love you.'

She kissed him back. 'I love you too and I do want

to marry you and I do want to live with you for ever and perhaps have babies, I do, honestly, I do want that, but, Mark, really, it's not going to be easy trying fitting everything in—'

'If you let me, I'm going to teach you some more,' he said softly, unravelling her towel, 'about prioritising. I'm going to teach you about time management and about optimising working hours and about living life the way it's supposed to be lived.'

'If I let you?' She blinked at him, startled by the meekness of that. 'If I *let* you? Where did that come from?'

'I'm not going to let myself get frustrated by you any more,' he said lightly. 'Life's too short already. I know I've got you now so I can have patience.'

'I'll believe that when I see it,' she murmured. 'I suppose living with you won't be so bad. I suppose. I suppose I could get used to being lazy.' She laughed when he pinched her gently.

'Organised,' he growled. 'I'm not talking lazy. The secret is organisation.'

Kate wrinkled her nose. She kissed the raspy edge of his cheek when he lifted her roughly into his arms and carried her back to the bedroom. 'You might not be frustrated but you're still a very bossy man, Mark Summers.'

'Katie, my love, you've always been in desperate need of decent bossing.'

Kate sunk her teeth into his ear lobe in gentle punishment. 'Kate,' she murmured. 'From now on, I warn you, my darling love, when you call me Katie, I'm going to bite you.'

But instead of seeming alarmed, Mark just laughed.

'Katie, Katie, Katie,' he taunted fearlessly, tumbling her down onto her bed and rolling her over, covering her mouth with his as they sank back into the covers. 'My sweet, vicious, ''Kissing''-scented Katie.'

READER SERVICE™

The best romantic fiction direct to your door

Our guarantee to you...

The Reader Service involves you in no obligation
to purchase, and is truly a service to you!

There are many extra benefits including a free
monthly Newsletter with author interviews,
book previews and much more.

Your books are sent direct to your door
on 14 days no obligation home approval.

We offer huge discounts on selected books
exclusively for subscribers.

Plus, we have a dedicated Customer Care team
on hand to answer all your queries on
(UK) 020 8288 2888
(Ireland) 01 278 2062.

MILLS & BOON®

*M*akes
any time
special

Enjoy a romantic novel from
Mills & Boon®

Presents...™ *Enchanted*™ TEMPTATION

Historical Romance™ ⅄MEDICAL ROMANCE™

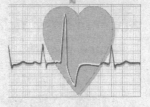

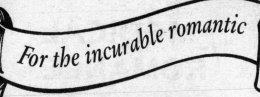

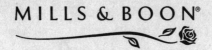